FIVE REASONS Y
A KALLE BLOMKVIST
 **MYSTERY**

Move over Sherlock Holmes. Hit the road
Hercule Poirot. Kalle Blomkvist is on the case!

All the thrills of a detective mystery,
but with plenty of laughs too

A twisting turning plot packed with
intriguing clues

Can you see what the evidence is pointing to?

Will Kalle Blomkvist catch his first killer?

LEARN TO SPEAK ROBBER LANGUAGE

Kalle Blomkvist and his friends have a secret language called Robber. It's really quite simple to crack when it's written down—every consonant is doubled, with an o put in between. Like this:

Ror-o-bob-bob-e-ror lol-a-non-gog-u-a-gog-e.

Robber language.

But when you speak Robber it sounds like complete gobbledygook, the key is to try and speak as quickly as you can. Try practising with these phrases and see if you can master them:

Wow-e-lol-lol coc-o-mom-e a-non-dod ror-e-sos-coc-u-e yoy-o-u sos-o-o-non.

We'll come and rescue you soon.

Dod-o-non-tot wow-o-ror-ror-yoy.
Pop-o-lol-i-coc-e o-non tot-hoh-e
wow-a-yoy.

Don't worry. Police on the way.

Wow-a-tot-coc-hoh o-u-tot.
Mom-u-ror-dod-e-ror-e-ror!

Watch out. Murderer!

Sos-o lol-o-non-gog, tot-u-ror-non-i-pop
hoh-e-a-dod.

So long, turnip head.

Lol-o-non-gog lol-i-vov-e tot-hoh-e
Wow-hoh-i-tot-e Ror-o-sos-e-sos!

Long live the White Roses!

OXFORD
UNIVERSITY PRESS

Great Clarendon Street, Oxford OX2 6DP
Oxford University Press is a department of the University of Oxford.
It furthers the University's objective of excellence in research, scholarship,
and education by publishing worldwide. Oxford is a registered trade mark
of Oxford University Press in the UK and in certain other countries

Text © copyright Saltkråkan AB/Astrid Lindgren 1946
First published in Sweden as *Mästerdetektiven Blomkvist* by Rabén & Sjögren, 1946
Translated from the Swedish by Susan Beard
English Translation © Susan Beard 2017
This edition first published 2017

British Library Cataloguing in Publication Data

Data available

ISBN: 978-0-19-274929-1

1 3 5 7 9 10 8 6 4 2

Printed in Great Britain

Paper used in the production of this book is a natural,
recyclable product made from wood grown in sustainable forests.
The manufacturing process conforms to the environmental
regulations of the country of origin.

A KALLE BLOMKVIST MYSTERY

LIVING DANGEROUSLY

Astrid Lindgren

Translated by Susan Beard

OXFORD
UNIVERSITY PRESS

'You're mad,' said Anders. 'Seriously, you must be mad. You're not lying there daydreaming again, are you?'

Kalle immediately leapt up from the lawn and glared from under his blonde fringe at his two friends standing by the fence. He felt insulted.

'Honestly, Kalle,' said Eva-Lotta. 'You'll get pressure sores if you lie under that pear tree every single day of the summer, staring into space.'

'I don't stare into space every day,' Kalle said angrily.

'Yes, Eva-Lotta, don't exaggerate,' said Anders. 'Remember that Sunday at the beginning of June? Kalle didn't lie under the pear tree once. And he wasn't playing detectives, either. Thieves and murderers could get away with—well, murder.'

'Oh yes, I remember now,' said Eva-Lotta. 'Murderers actually had a Sunday off at the beginning of June.'

'Oh, get lost,' said Kalle.

'Yep, that's just what we were planning to do,' said Anders. 'But we wanted you to come with us. If you think the crooks can manage without you for an hour or so, that is.'

'Oh, I'm sure they can't,' said Eva-Lotta, grinning. 'They're like babies. You can't take your eyes off them for a second.'

Kalle sighed. It was hopeless, absolutely hopeless. He was Master Detective Blomkvist, and he demanded respect for his profession. But did he get it? Not from Anders and Eva-Lotta, at least, even though he had single-handedly caught three jewellery thieves last summer. Anders and Eva-Lotta had helped a bit, but it was he, Kalle, with his quick wits and powers of observation who had tracked the villains down.

Then Anders and Eva-Lotta had realized he was a detective all right, one who could do his job. But now they were teasing him as if it had never happened! As if there were no criminals at all in the whole wide world, and you didn't need to be constantly on the lookout. As if Kalle was simply an overexcited turnip head with a vivid imagination.

'You weren't quite so smug last summer,' he said, and sent a long, indignant stream of spit over the grass. 'What about that time we nabbed the jewellery thieves? I didn't hear anyone complain about Master Detective Blomkvist then.'

'And no one's complaining about you now, either,' said Anders. 'But don't you get it? That kind of thing only happens once, and never again. This little town has existed since thirteen-hundred and something, and up to now there have never been any criminals here apart from those jewellery thieves, as far as I know. That was a year ago, but you're still sprawling under that pear tree, solving crimes! Give up, Kalle, give up! Believe me, there won't be any more crooks around here for ages.'

'Everything has its time, you know,' said Eva-Lotta. 'There's a time for hunting down crooks, and there's a time for making mincemeat of the Reds.'

'Talking of mincemeat,' said Anders, enthusiastically. 'The Red Roses are up for a battle again. Benka came with their declaration of war just now. Read for yourself!'

He pulled a large, rolled-up piece of paper out of his pocket and handed it to Kalle, who read:

WAR! WAR!
To the crackpot leader of the gang of hooligans who call themselves the White Roses.
Herewith we make it known that there is not a farmer in all of Sweden with a pig half as brainless as the leader of the White Roses. Yesterday we had proof! This scum of humanity met the mighty and honourable leader of the Red Roses in the town square. The said scum did not stand aside but in

*his stupendous ignorance shoved our noble
and peace-loving leader out of the way and
shouted foul abuse. This offence can only be
washed clean with blood.*

*Now the Red and the White Roses do battle,
and it shall send a thousand souls to death
and deadly night.*

Sixten,
Knight and Leader of the Red Roses

'We'll soon sort them out,' said Anders. 'Are you coming with us?'

Kalle grinned happily. The Roses battles, which had raged for many years with only a few short breaks in between, weren't something you turned down willingly. They were thrilling and gave them something to look forward to in the summer holidays, which could otherwise have been a bit monotonous. Cycling and swimming, watering the strawberries, running errands for his dad's grocery shop, sitting on the riverbank with a fishing rod, hanging around in Eva-Lotta's garden, and kicking a ball about—that wasn't enough to fill the days. After all, the summer holidays were so long.

Yes, luckily the summer holidays *were* long, and the best invention ever, according to Kalle. It was quite strange to think that it was adults who had come up with the idea, and that they actually allowed you to roam around in the summer sunshine for two and a half months and not bother your head a jot about The Thirty Years' War and stuff like that! You could spend your time fighting the battles of the Roses instead. That was much nicer.

'What do you mean, am I coming?' said Kalle. 'Do you even have to ask?'

Criminals had been few and far between lately, and Master Detective Blomkvist was only too happy to take some time off to concentrate on the technicalities of war, which the Roses had developed through their confrontations. And it would be interesting to see what the Reds had cooked up this time.

'I think I'll set off on a little tour of reconnaissance,' said Anders.

'You do that,' said Eva-Lotta. 'We'll start in half an hour. I've got knives to sharpen first.'

That sounded impressive, and dangerous. Anders and Kalle nodded in approval. Eva-Lotta was a warrior you could depend on.

The knives that had to be sharpened were in fact only Mr Lisander the baker's bread knives, but even so! Eva-Lotta had promised her dad to turn the grinding wheel for him before she set off. It was a sweaty job, standing in the scorching hot July sunshine and turning the heavy wheel. It made it a whole lot easier if you imagined you were toiling over the weapons necessary for war with the Roses. 'And it shall send a thousand souls to death and deadly night,' muttered Eva-Lotta to herself, as she stood beside the grinding wheel and turned the handle until the sweat poured off her forehead and her blonde hair glued itself to her face.

'What did you say?' asked Mr Lisander, looking up from the wheel.

'Nothing.'

'Then that was probably what I heard,' said Mr Lisander, testing the sharpness of the breadknife against his finger. 'You run along now!'

And that's what Eva-Lotta did. She slipped quickly through the gap in the fence that divided her garden from Kalle's. There was a plank missing in one place. It had been missing for as long as anyone could remember, and it could go on being missing as far as Kalle and Eva-Lotta were concerned. They needed that shortcut.

Sometimes Mr Blomkvist the grocer, who liked things to be done properly, said to Mr Lisander the baker, as they sat among Mr Lisander's lilac bushes on a summer's evening:

'You know, old chap, I think we should mend that fence. It looks a bit untidy.'

'Oh, I think we can wait until the kids are big enough to get stuck in the gap,' said the baker.

Despite non-stop bun eating Eva-Lotta remained as

thin as a rake, and it was no problem at all for her to get through the narrow opening.

There was whistling outside on the road. Anders, leader of the White Roses, had returned from his tour of reconnaissance.

'They're in their headquarters,' he yelled. 'Forward to battle and victory!'

Kalle had resumed his position under the pear tree after Eva-Lotta disappeared to the grinding wheel and Anders on his spying mission. He used this short interval before war broke out to have an important conversation.

Yes, he had a conversation, even though not a living thing could be seen in the vicinity. It was with a close friend, one he'd had for many years. Oh, what a wonderful person he was, this eager listener! He treated the detective with the deep respect he so well deserved and almost never got from anyone else, least of all Anders and Eva-Lotta. Right now he was sitting at the master's feet, hanging on every word.

'Anders Bengtsson and Eva-Lotta Lisander are seriously nonchalant when it comes to criminality in our society,' Detective Blomkvist declared, looking into the eyes of his listener. 'One period of calm and they stop being vigilant. They simply don't understand that calm is deceptive.'

'Is it?' asked the imaginary listener, sounding absolutely terrified.

'Calm is deceptive,' repeated the master detective emphatically. 'This delightful town, this glorious summer sunshine, this idyllic tranquillity—tosh! It can all change in an instant. Criminality can cast its evil shadow over us at any minute.'

The imaginary listener gasped.

'Mr Blomkvist, you're scaring me,' he said, throwing glances to left and right, as if criminal goings-on were lurking round the next corner.

'Leave everything to me,' said the master detective. 'Don't worry! I'm keeping watch.'

The imaginary listener was so grateful he could hardly speak. His stammered thanks were interrupted by a war cry from Anders on the other side of the gate.

'Forward to battle and victory!'

Master Detective Blomkvist shot up as if a wasp had stung him. It wouldn't do to be found under the pear tree again.

'Farewell,' he said to his imaginary listener, and he had a feeling this farewell would be for a long time. The Wars of the Roses meant there wouldn't be many spare minutes for discussing criminal exploits on the lawn. And that was just as well. To be completely honest, you had a hard job finding villains in this town. A whole year since last time, imagine that! Another skirmish between the Roses was certainly welcome!

His pretend listener looked anxiously as he watched him go.

'Farewell,' the master detective said again. 'I've been called up for military service. But don't worry! I shouldn't think anything serious will happen just yet.'

Shouldn't think! Shouldn't think!? There he is, the master detective, running off when he should be keeping watch over security in the town. Off he goes, whistling cheerfully, and his bare brown feet thud against the garden path as he hurries off to Anders and Eva-Lotta.

Shouldn't think! You've got it wrong this time, Mr Master Detective!

In this town there is only one main street and one back street, so Mr Lisander the baker usually explained to visitors. And the baker was right. Storgatan and Lillgatan, that was all there was, plus the main square. The rest of the town was made up of narrow, cobbled, bumpy alleyways, or streets that either came to a dead end at the river or unexpectedly stopped at some ramshackle old building which, because of its age, stubbornly blocked any modern town planning. On the edge of town there were some newer bungalows with neat gardens, but they were an exception. Most of the gardens were like the baker's: more or less overgrown and with knobbly old apple and pear trees, and scruffy lawns that needed cutting. Most of the houses were like the baker's, too: large, rambling wooden places which, in a giddy burst of artistic inspiration, a builder in times gone by had adorned with the most unexpected corners, towers and turrets. The town certainly couldn't be called beautiful, but it had a comforting, old-fashioned tranquillity. And perhaps it was beautiful, after all, especially on a warm July day like today, when the roses, peonies, and sweet-smelling stocks were flowering in every garden, and Lillgatan's lime trees were reflected in the river as it meandered gently along.

As Kalle, Anders and Eva-Lotta came striding along the riverbank on their way to the Red Roses' headquarters, they didn't care if the town was beautiful or not. The only thing they knew was that it made an excellent battleground for the Wars of the Roses. There were nooks and crannies to hide in, fences to climb over, narrow, twisting alleyways useful for shaking off pursuers, rooftops to clamber over and garden outhouses to barricade yourself in. As long as a town had all these brilliant advantages it didn't need to be beautiful. It was enough that the sun was shining and the paving stones felt warm under their bare feet. They felt as if their bodies were bursting with summer. The slightly stagnant smell of the river, mixed in with the perfume of the roses from someone's garden close by, was lovely and summery too. And the ice-cream kiosk on the street corner was the only added extra the town needed, according to Kalle, Anders and Eva-Lotta. They didn't need any other attractions.

They bought an ice cream each and continued along the road. Down by the bridge Constable Björk was out on patrol, making his way slowly towards them. His uniform buttons glinted in the sunshine.

'Hello, Constable Björk,' shouted Eva-Lotta.

'Well, hello there,' the police officer said. 'And hello, Master Detective,' he added, patting Kalle's shoulder. 'Any new cases today?'

Kalle looked offended. Hadn't Constable Björk taken part in Kalle's hunt for the jewellery thieves last summer, and shared the glory when they were caught? Well then, he of all people had no reason to be making jokes.

'Nope, not today at least,' Anders answered for Kalle. 'Every thief and murderer has been given orders to put their dodgy dealings on hold until tomorrow, because Kalle hasn't got time for them today.'

'No, today we've decided to cut the Red Roses' ears off,' said Eva-Lotta, smiling prettily at Constable Björk. She liked him a lot.

'Eva-Lotta, sometimes I have a feeling you ought to be a little more ladylike,' said Constable Björk, looking down in concern at the thin, suntanned Amazon who was standing in the gutter, trying to pick up an empty cigarette packet between her toes. She succeeded, and with a sharp flick of her foot tossed the cigarette packet into the river.

'Ladylike? Yes, on Mondays,' Eva-Lotta assured him, her whole face lighting up in a smile. 'See you later, Constable Björk. Got to dash.'

Constable Björk shook his head and wandered on.

It was very tempting, crossing the bridge. Naturally, you could walk across it in the normal fashion, but there were railings on each side, fairly narrow ones, and if you crossed the bridge by balancing on top of the wall you could give yourself a few minutes of absolute stomach-churning scariness due to the possibility of plummeting into the water at any second. Admittedly it hadn't happened so far, despite lots of railing-balancing attempts, but you never knew for sure. And even though cutting off the Red Roses' ears was pretty urgent business, Kalle, Anders and Eva-Lotta all thought they had time for a little balancing. This was, of course, strictly forbidden, but Constable Björk had disappeared and there was no one else around.

Actually, there was one person. Just as they had climbed bravely on to the railings and the fluttery feeling had started as expected, old Mr Gren came toddling along from the other end of the bridge. But they didn't have to worry about old Gren. He stopped beside the children, sighed as he always did, and said in his usual absent-minded way:

'Ah yes, the happy games of childhood! Childhood's happy, innocent games. Ah yes!'

That's what old Gren always said. They copied him sometimes. Never so that he could hear, of course. But when Kalle kicked a football through his dad's shop window by mistake, or when Anders came off his bike and fell head first into a nettle patch, Eva-Lotta could be heard to say:

'Ah yes, the happy games of childhood. Ah yes.'

Luckily, they reached the other side of the bridge. No one had fallen in this time, either. Anders usually looked around to see if anyone had spotted their antics, but Lillgatan was still deserted, apart from old Gren toddling off in the distance. You couldn't mistake the way he walked.

'I don't know anyone who's got such a strange walk as old Gren,' said Anders.

'It's not just his walk. Gren is strange all over,' said Kalle. 'But perhaps you do go strange when you live all alone.'

'Poor thing,' said Eva-Lotta. 'Imagine living in that run-down old place with no one to clean for you, or make you food or anything.'

'Huh, you can manage without cleaning,' said Anders, after careful consideration. 'And I wouldn't mind living alone for a while. At least then I could build my models in peace.'

For people like Anders, who had to live among masses of younger brothers and sisters in a miniscule flat, there was nothing particularly off-putting about having an entire house all to yourself.

'Oh, you'd go strange within a week,' said Kalle. 'Stranger than you already are, I mean. As strange as old Gren.'

'My dad doesn't like old Gren,' said Eva-Lotta. 'He says Gren is a loan shark.'

Anders and Kalle didn't know what that meant, so Eva-Lotta explained.

'Dad says a loan shark is someone who lends money to people who need it.'

'Well, that's very considerate of him,' said Anders.

'No, it's not,' said Eva-Lotta. 'It's like this. Say you've got to borrow one krona. That you absolutely, desperately need twenty-five ören for something.'

'A bar of chocolate,' suggested Kalle.

'You said it,' said Anders. 'I feel a need for that already.'

'Then you go to Gren,' said Eva-Lotta. 'Or some other loan shark. And he gives you the twenty-five ören...'

'Does he?' said Anders. He was pleasantly surprised at this possibility.

'Yes, but you've got to promise to pay him back a month later,' said Eva-Lotta. 'And you can't just repay the twenty-five ören. You've got to give him fifty.'

'That won't happen,' said Anders. 'Why would I do that?'

'Honestly, Anders, have you never done percentages in school?' said Eva-Lotta. 'Gren wants interest on his money, don't you get it?'

'Yes, but he could be reasonable,' said Kalle, who didn't want to see Anders' finances go entirely down the drain.

'That's exactly what loan sharks *aren't*,' said Eva-Lotta. 'They charge too much interest, and it's against the law. That's why Dad doesn't like Gren.'

'Then why are people such twits that they borrow from a loan shark in the first place?' Kalle asked. 'They could borrow money for chocolate from someone else.'

'Chump,' said Eva-Lotta. 'It not always a question of twenty-five ören for chocolate. It could be thousands of kronor. Maybe there are people who are desperate for five thousand kronor that very minute, and perhaps no one else can lend it to them. No one apart from loan sharks like Gren, that is.'

'Forget about old Gren,' said Anders, leader of the White Roses. 'Forward to battle and victory!'

They had reached the postmaster's house and in the back garden was an outhouse that doubled as a garage and the headquarters of the Red Roses, because the postmaster's son Sixten was the leader of this war-like gang.

It so happened the garage was empty and abandoned for the time being. From far away they could see a notice pinned to the door. It would have been a simple matter to walk right in through the garden gate and up to the garage to read what was written on the notice, but that was not how the battles of the Roses were fought. It could be a trap. Perhaps the Red Roses were lying in wait inside their locked headquarters, ready to hurl themselves at any unsuspecting people who dared to come near.

The leader of the White Roses instructed his troops.

'Kalle, you sneak along the hedge until you get behind

the headquarters, out of sight of the enemy. Climb up on to the roof and bring back the proclamation, dead or alive!'

'"The proclamation dead or alive"—what do you mean?' asked Kalle.

'Shut up,' said Anders. 'You're the one who'll be dead or alive, not the proclamation. Eva-Lotta, stay here, lie very still and keep watch through the hedge. If you notice Kalle is in danger, whistle our signal.'

'What about you?' asked Eva-Lotta. 'What will you do?'

'I'll go in and ask Sixten's mum if she knows where he is,' said Anders.

They all did as Anders said. Kalle soon reached the headquarters. Getting up on the roof was no problem, he had done that many times before. It was only a matter of squeezing through the hedge and climbing on top of the dustbin that stood behind the garage.

He made his way over the roof as quietly as he possibly could, so the enemy wouldn't hear him. He knew very well the garage was empty—Eva-Lotta knew it too—but Anders knew it more than anyone because he had gone and asked for Sixten at the postmaster's house. But the Wars of the Roses had their own very special rules. That's why Kalle crawled across the roof as if he was on a hugely dangerous mission, and Eva-Lotta lay behind the hedge tensely following his every move, ready to whistle the signal if, against all odds, it should be needed.

At that moment Anders returned. Sixten's mum had no idea where her precious son could be.

Kalle leaned carefully over the edge of the roof, and stretching down as far as he could he grabbed the notice on the door. Then calmly and silently he slithered back the way he had come. Eva-Lotta kept watch over him to the very last minute.

'Well done, courageous warrior,' said Anders approvingly, as Kalle handed him the proclamation. 'Now we'll see!'

Sixten, 'Nobleman and Leader of the White Roses', was the author of this strange proclamation. They had to admit the language was particularly bad to have been written by a 'nobleman'. You would expect something more refined from a man of noble birth.

You filthy vermin! Yes, you, Red Roses, who contaminate this town with your stinking presence. Herewith we state that we, the honourable White Roses, have scarpered to the battlefield on the Prairie. Come here instantly so we can eliminate those disgusting weeds what call themselves the White Roses, and scatter their ashes in Johansson's manure heap where they belong.

Come on, you foul vermin!!!

No one reading these affectionate words would ever

guess that the White and Red Roses were in fact best friends. Apart from Kalle and Eva-Lotta, Sixten was Anders' most reliable friend, not counting Benka and Jonte that is, who were also pretty decent Red Roses. And if there was anyone in this town that Sixten, Benka and Jonte liked above all others, it was those filthy vermin Anders, Kalle and Eva-Lotta.

'That's done it!' said Anders, when he had finished reading. 'To the Prairie! Forward to battle and victory!'

It was good the Prairie existed—good, that is, for those generations of children who had played there for as long as anyone could remember. Many a steady, dependable father felt sentimental when they recalled their childhood games on the Prairie. Children from later generations could use that to their advantage. If Kalle came home one evening with a ripped shirt after a particularly lively battle, Mr Blomkvist the grocer never commented because it brought to mind a shirt that was torn to shreds on the Prairie one spring evening about thirty years before. And even if Mrs Lisander would have preferred her young daughter to make friends with other girls her age, instead of racketing around with the boys out on the Prairie, it wasn't worth her while objecting, because the baker would only look at her knowingly and say:

'And when you were young, Mia, which little lass was always out playing on the Prairie?'

The Prairie was a piece of open land on the edge of

town. It was covered in the kind of short grass that was fun to run about on with bare feet. Every spring it was bright green and bouncy, and the whole Prairie turned into a hummocky green sea with splashes of yellow from masses of coltsfoot flowers. But the summer sun had been harsh and now the Prairie grass was brown and dried-up. Kalle, Anders and Eva-Lotta, who had hurried to take up Sixten's irresistible challenge, stared over the battlefield, their eyes squinting in the sun. They were on the lookout for their enemies but there was no sign of the Red Roses. Much of the Prairie was covered in shrubby undergrowth and juniper bushes, which made very good hiding places for a stealthy Red Rose.

The Whites let out their terrifying war cry and plunged in among the bushes. They searched under every bramble, they poked and prodded, but there was no enemy there. They carried on until they reached the far side of the Prairie, all the way to the old Mansion, but it was no good.

'What kind of stupid joke is this?' said Anders. 'They're not here anywhere.'

Then across the stillness of the Prairie rang out the piercing, mocking laughter of three voices.

'No, it can't be,' said Eva-Lotta, looking around nervously. 'Do you know, I think they've got inside the Mansion.

'Yes, they really have,' said Kalle, admiringly.

On the edge of the Prairie, standing among aspen trees with their quivering leaves, was an old house known as the Mansion. It was an elegant house, at least 200 years old, but it had seen better days. Now, out of a window at the rear of the Mansion, stuck three triumphant faces.

'Woe to anyone who approaches the new headquarters of the Red Roses!' shouted Sixten.

'How on earth ... ?' said Anders.

'Wouldn't you like to know!' shouted Sixten. 'The door was open. It was as easy as that.'

The Mansion had been empty for many years and was very run down. Long ago the town council had decided to restore it and move it to the city park and turn it into a local history museum. This would be paid for by donations, so the council had planned, but the money was slow coming in and all the while the Mansion was becoming more and more dilapidated. Up to now it had been kept locked and out of bounds for the youngsters of the town. Now that the rotting door could no longer keep trespassers out, it was necessary for the town council to do something about it very quickly, while there was still something left to put in a local history museum. Judging from the racket the Reds were making inside the ancient walls, they weren't exactly treating their surroundings with respect. The old floorboards groaned anxiously under their lively feet, which thudded about their new headquarters in wild leaps of joy.

'We'll capture the scum and lock them in here and let them starve to death,' said Sixten jubilantly.

His future victims came running expectantly towards their fate, and the Reds did nothing to stop them. Sixten had decided the Reds would hold the top floor, to the death if necessary, because it was easier to defend. A sweeping staircase led to the upstairs, and there in the middle of it stood the Reds, and judging from their wild gestures nothing would make them happier than setting about their enemies.

The Whites went boldly to attack, and the commotion and crashing that took place when the warriors met would have been enough to make the members of the Local History Museum Association tear out their hair, had they heard it. Their future museum was trembling at the joints, and the swirling wooden banisters of the staircase sagged alarmingly. Wild cries rose up to the beautiful old plaster ceiling, and the leader of the White Roses travelled backwards down the stairs with a noise that must have made the spirits of past residents, assuming there were any, turn even paler and huddle together in fear in the corners.

The success of the battle ebbed and flowed. One minute the Whites were driving their opponents back almost to the top of the staircase, and the next they found themselves having to back down in a disorganized retreat towards the ground floor. When the battle had flowed backwards and forwards for easily half an hour, everyone involved began to long for a change. The Whites drew back for a moment to prepare for their final, devastating attack. That was when Sixten gave his troops a swift, silent order. The next second, and completely without warning, the Reds left their position on the stairs and retreated at lightning speed to the top floor. Sixten and his gang knew there were many possibilities for hiding away in rooms and wardrobes up here, because they had carefully inspected the entire building earlier in the day. And when Anders, Kalle and Eva-Lotta came storming up the stairs it was as if the Red Roses had gone up in a puff of smoke. They had made good use of their few seconds' start and at that moment were barricaded inside a conveniently-sited wardrobe, watching through a crack as the Whites held a hurried conference right outside.

'Spread out,' said the Whites' leader. 'Drive the enemy from whatever hole he has found to hide in, trembling for his life! And when you find him, make the process short.'

The Red Roses, inside the wardrobe, grew smug when they heard this. Sixten's eyes glinted happily through the crack in the door. But the Whites knew nothing about this.

Spread out, their leader had said. That was the most idiotic thing he could have thought up. It sealed his fate.

He spread himself out immediately and disappeared round a corner.

As soon as he was out of sight, Kalle and Eva-Lotta crept cautiously in the opposite direction. There was a door here, and they opened it. Inside was a beautiful, sunlit room, and even though they could see that the enemy wasn't inside, they went in anyway, to give themselves a short break from the fighting and to look out of the window. But this proved to be a seriously wrong move.

They headed back to the door just in time to hear a key turning on the outside, and the Red leader's cruel laughter and horrible cry of victory:

'Hah! You've had your chips now, you vermin! You won't get out of here alive.'

And then Benka's screech:

'Yes, you'll have to sit here until you're covered in moss. But we'll come and visit you at Christmas. What presents would you like?'

'Your heads on a platter,' shouted Eva-Lotta from inside.

'Stuffed with an apple, like they do with all pigs' heads,' added Kalle.

'Bad mannered to the end,' the Reds' leader said sadly to his comrades. Then he raised his voice and shouted to the prisoners:

'Is there a final message you'd like us to pass on to your loved ones?'

'Yes, ask my dad to phone the young offenders' institution and tell them where they can come and collect you,' said Eva-Lotta.

'Bye bye, you mongrels,' said Sixten. 'Shout when you're hungry and we'll bring you a bone to chew.'

Then he turned to Benka and Jonte, gleefully rubbing his hands together.

'And now, my brave fellow warriors, somewhere in this house at this very moment is a miserable little rat calling itself the leader of the White Roses. Alone and helpless! Find him! Find him, I say!'

The Reds did their best. They tiptoed down the long corridor that ran the entire length of the top floor. They peered inside every room. They stood and waited outside wardrobe doors. They knew that wherever the Whites' leader was, he must surely be aware of the terrible danger facing him. His comrades were locked in. He was alone against the three of them. Three warriors with a burning desire to get hold of him, because according to the battles of the Roses, capturing the other gang's leader was an amazing act of bravado more or less as if the Americans had captured Hitler during World War Two and imprisoned him in Sing-Sing jail.

But the leader of the Whites had hidden himself well. There was no trace of him, however hard the Reds searched. Until, that is, Sixten suddenly heard a very faint creak above his head.

'He's up in the loft,' he whispered.

'You mean there's a loft here?' said Jonte in surprise. The Red Roses hadn't found it, even though they had searched the house thoroughly earlier in the day. But perhaps that wasn't so strange, because the door to the narrow staircase up to the loft was an ordinary door covered in wallpaper and would hardly be noticed unless you knew it was there. And it took the Reds a good while to find it.

But after that things happened fast. Admittedly Anders was waiting up in the loft, fully prepared for battle, loudly warning anyone who hadn't written their last will and testament not to come anywhere near him, but that didn't help.

Sixten, who was unusually big and strong for his age, took the lead, assisted by Benka and Jonte when necessary, and Anders was pulled, struggling wildly, down the stairs and away to an unknown fate.

Kalle and Eva-Lotta shouted words of comfort to him through their locked door.

'Wow-e-lol-lol coc-o-mom-e a-non-dod ror-e-sos-coc-u-e yoy-o-u sos-o-o-non,' they yelled.

That meant 'We'll come and rescue you soon' in the secret language the White Roses used. They knew there was no better way to annoy the Reds, who had tried for ages to work out the weird language the Whites had mastered to perfection, and could rattle off so insanely fast that it sounded like gobbledygook to anyone who didn't have a clue what it meant. Sixten, Benka and Jonte had never seen it written down, otherwise they wouldn't have had the slightest difficulty working out the code: every consonant was doubled and an 'o' put in between. So, for example, Kalle became Kok-a-lol-lol-e, and Anders A-non-dod-e-ror-sos.

It was Eva-Lotta who had told them about the language, the so-called Robber language, that her father had passed on to her. One evening, quite by chance, the baker had told her that when he and his friends were lads they used to speak this language when they didn't want anyone else to know what they were saying. Eva-Lotta's fervent enthusiasm for the Robber language surprised her dad, because he had never noticed any enthusiasm on her part when it came to German verbs and such like, but he very kindly sat with her the whole evening, helping her practise, and the next day she passed on her knowledge to Anders and Kalle.

One of the reasons the Reds battled with the Whites was to make the Whites part with the key to this secret code. Another reason, an even more important one, was to win back the Great Stonytotem. The Great Stonytotem was a very grand name for a rather insignificant object. The Great Stonytotem was, in fact, a stone, an odd-shaped stone that Benka had found. If you were feeling generous you could say it was shaped like a little old man sitting down and staring at his navel, like the Buddha. The Reds immediately made it their special trophy, and gave it mighty powers. That was enough for the Whites to feel it was their sacred duty to get hold of it at all costs. The fiercest battles of all had raged over the Great Stonytotem. It might seem odd that so much importance was attached to a small stone, but why shouldn't the Red Roses love their stone as much as the Scots loved their Stone of Destiny, and were as deeply upset when the Whites craftily helped themselves to it as the Scottish were when the English placed the stone in Westminster Abbey?

It was a painful fact that the Whites currently had possession of the Great Stonytotem and were keeping it hidden somewhere. It would have been a simple thing to hide it in a place where no living soul could find it, but one very particular rule of the Wars of the Roses was that whoever had possession of the stone had a duty to give their opponents at least one clue to help them find it. The clue could be in the form of a map—a very hard to read and partly misleading one—or a riddle scrawled on a slip of paper and pushed one dark night through the enemy's letter box. From that you could use all your available brain power to deduce that the Great Stonytotem was hidden in the empty crow's nest in the elm tree growing in the most northerly corner of the churchyard, or under a tile on the roof of shoemaker Bengtsson's log shed.

Right now it was in neither of those places. Right now it was in an entirely different place. And one of the main reasons the Wars of the Roses had flared up again on this fiendishly hot July day was because the Reds were desperate to know exactly where this place was. Now the Whites' leader had been taken hostage, it might not be entirely impossible to find out.

'We'll come and rescue you soon,' was what Kalle and Eva-Lotta had called out. And their leader was certainly in need of some encouragement, because at this very moment strong arms were carrying him off for an agonising interrogation about the Great Stonytotem and the secret language.

'I wow-o-non-tot tot-e-lol-lol tot-hoh-e-mom,' Anders promised heroically at the top of his voice as he passed the locked door his fellow warriors were trapped behind.

'Just you wait, you won't be tot-totting much longer,' said Sixten threateningly, holding Anders' arm even tighter. 'We'll get it out of you, don't you worry.'

'Be strong! Resist!' shouted Kalle.

'Don't give in! We're coming soon,' shouted Eva-Lotta.

And through the door they heard their leader's final, proud words:

'Long live the White Roses!'

And after that:

'Let go of my arm! I'll go with you willingly. I am prepared, gentlemen!'

After that they heard nothing. A great silence fell over their prison. The enemy had left the house and taken their leader with them.

4

It was true the Reds had hinted that Kalle and Eva-Lotta would have to stay where they were until they were covered in moss, but they didn't mean it literally. Even in the Wars of the Roses they had to make allowances for those annoying, obstructive elements called parents. Of course, it was an incredible nuisance when noble warriors had to pause in the middle of the most frenzied battle to go home and eat shepherd's pie and rhubarb crumble, but parents had the idea that kids should stick to dinner times. It was an accepted part of the Wars of the Roses that you had to submit to your parents' idiotic demands. If you didn't, there was a risk the fighting would be seriously interrupted. Parents had such a pathetic lack of imagination that you could quite easily be grounded on the very evening put aside for a battle that would clinch possession of the Great Stonytotem. Parents knew painfully little about the Great Stonytotem, despite the fact that their own childhood memories were an occasional glimmer of light that shone on their limited ability to understand.

When the Reds took off with Anders, leaving Kalle and Eva-Lotta to die of starvation locked inside an empty room in an uninhabited mansion, it really only meant they would starve for two hours, in other words until seven o' clock. At seven o'clock a large nutritious dinner would be served in the home of Mr Blomkvist the grocer and Mr Lisander the baker, as well as every other family in town. In plenty of time before this crucial strike of the clock, Sixten would send either Benka or Jonte to creep in and silently unlock the door. So Kalle and Eva-Lotta were very relaxed as they stared starvation in the face. But it was a terrific blunder to have been locked up like this, and it also meant a whopping victory on points for the Reds. Their upper hand at the moment, after capturing the Whites' leader, was truly catastrophic. Not even the fact that the Whites had possession of the Great Stonytotem could beat that.

Eva-Lotta looked bitterly out of the window as Anders was led away. There they went, the White leader surrounded by his enemies. They marched over the sun-baked Prairie towards the town. Soon they would be out of sight.

'I wonder where they're planning to take him,' said Eva-Lotta.

'To Sixten's garage, of course,' said Kalle, and added, anxiously, 'If only I had a newspaper or something!'

'A newspaper,' said Eva-Lotta, irritably. 'You want to

read the paper now, when we should be trying to get out of here?"

'You're absolutely right,' said Kalle. 'We must get out of here. And that's why I want a newspaper.'

'Did you think it would have an article telling you the best way to climb down walls?'

Eva-Lotta leaned out of the window to estimate the distance to the ground.

'We'll smash ourselves to a pulp if we jump,' she went on. 'But that can't be helped.'

Kalle gave a satisfied whistle.

'The wallpaper. I never thought of that. It'll do nicely.'

Quickly he ripped off a strip of the peeling wallpaper. Eva-Lotta looked at him, bewildered.

'I bet this was really beautiful wallpaper a few hundred years ago,' said Kalle. He bent down and pushed the paper under the gap in the door.

'Purely routine,' he said, taking his penknife from his pocket.

He folded out the smallest, thinnest blade and poked it carefully into the keyhole. There was a clink on the other side. It was the key, falling out of the lock and on to the floor.

Kalle pulled the wallpaper towards him, and sure enough, there lay the key. It had landed exactly where it should.

'As I said, purely routine,' said Master Detective

Blomkvist, suggesting to Eva-Lotta that his detective business forced him on a daily basis to open locked doors in one tricky way or another.

'Kalle, you're the best!' Eva-Lotta said in admiration.

Kalle unlocked the door. They were free.

'But we can't leave without saying sorry to the Reds,' Kalle said.

He found a stump of a pencil among the many things in his pocket and handed it to Eva-Lotta.

On the back of the wallpaper she wrote:

Red Roses, you corking great idiots!
Your attempt to cultivate moss has clearly failed. We have waited exactly five minutes and thirty seconds for it to start growing, but now we're off. You weedy little squirts, didn't you know the White Roses can walk through walls?'

They made sure the window was properly closed, then they locked the door from the outside and left the key in the keyhole. They left their farewell note on the door handle.

'That should give them something to think about. The window shut from the inside and the door locked—that'll really make them scratch their heads and wonder how we got out,' said Eva-Lotta joyfully.

'One point to the White Roses,' said Kalle.

Anders wasn't in Sixten's garage. Kalle and Eva-Lotta had carried out a very cautious expedition to find out the best way of freeing him, but the garage was as silent and empty as before.

Sixten's mum was in the garden, hanging washing on the line.

'Do you happen to know where Sixten is?' asked Eva-Lotta.

'He was here a minute ago,' said the Postmaster's wife. 'With Bengt, Anders and John.' She always called Benka and Jonte by their proper names.

Evidently the Reds had taken their captive somewhere more secure. But where?

The answer was right under their noses. Kalle saw it first. A penknife was rammed into the grass, holding down a small piece of paper. The knife belonged to Anders—Kalle and Eva-Lotta both recognized it. Written on the paper was one word only: Jonte.

In an unguarded moment the leader of the Whites had managed to leave this brief message to his fellow warriors.

Kalle frowned.

'Jonte,' he said. 'That can only mean one thing. Anders is imprisoned at Jonte's home.'

'Well yes, what else could it mean?' said Eva-Lotta. 'If he really is at Jonte's then of course the cleverest thing to write is 'Jonte' and not Benka, for example.'

Kalle didn't answer.

Jonte lived in the part of town known as Riffraff Hill. People living in the small ramshackle houses there did not exactly move in the upper circles of town society. But then Jonte never pretended to come from a better background. He was perfectly satisfied with his family's decrepit cottage, with its one room and kitchen on the ground floor and small attic room on the floor above. The attic could only be lived in during the summer. In the winter it was far too cold. But now it was July and the attic was as hot as a furnace, and that made it a suitably gruesome place for a painful interrogation. Jonte had sole use of the attic. He slept there on a camp bed and he had his own home-made shelf system of crates where he kept his detective magazines and his stamp collection and his other few prized worldly possessions. No king could have been happier in his palace than Jonte was in his little room, even though it was stifling hot and flies buzzed in the roof.

This was where the Reds had taken Anders, because as luck would have it Jonte's mum and dad were working on their allotment on the outskirts of town. They had a packed lunch with them and wouldn't be home for hours. Jonte had been left to look after himself, with sausages and potatoes to fry when he got hungry.

Seeing as Sixten's mum was hanging up washing outside the Reds' headquarters in Sixten's garage, and seeing as it was so wonderfully parent-free at Jonte's house, Sixten had come up with the brilliant idea of interrogating Anders in Jonte's attic room over on Riffraff Hill.

Kalle and Eva-Lotta had a conference. Naturally, they could start their rescue operation straight away, but after some consideration they thought it was wiser to wait. It would be stupid to reveal themselves to the Reds now. Soon it would be dinner time. Soon Sixten would be sending Benka or Jonte to the Mansion. And soon either Benka or Jonte would be standing there in total amazement over Kalle and Eva-Lotta's escape. That was a deeply satisfying thought. They had scored such a good point it would be a shame to spoil it.

So Kalle and Eva-Lotta decided to postpone the rescue operation until after dinner. They knew very well that Anders would be given permission on his honour to go home and eat too, and nothing can be more humiliating for a rescue bid than to arrive at the place just when the person who needs rescuing has left to go home and eat dinner.

'And by the way,' Kalle said. 'If you're going to spy on someone who's being held indoors, it's best to do it just as it's getting dark and people put their lights on. Before they close the curtains. Anyone who knows anything about criminal forensic work knows that.'

'Jonte hasn't got curtains,' said Eva-Lotta.

'So much the better,' said Kalle.

'But how are we going to spy through a window in an attic?' asked Eva-Lotta. 'I know I've got long legs but even so...'

'I can tell you haven't read anything about the technicalities of detective work,' said Kalle. 'What do you think detectives in Stockholm do? If they want to keep watch on a flat full of criminals on the third floor, they gain access to a flat on the other side of the street, preferably on the fourth floor so they are a bit higher up than the criminals. Then the police stand there with binoculars looking right in on the villains before they have closed the curtains.'

'If I was a criminal I'd close the curtains before putting on the light,' said Eva-Lotta, practical as ever. 'And anyway, which flat have you planned to gain access to so we can spy on Jonte?'

Kalle hadn't given that much thought. No doubt it was easier for detectives in Stockholm to get access to peoples' flats. All they had to do was show their badges. It was hardly likely to be as easy for Kalle and Eva-Lotta. Besides, there weren't any buildings opposite Jonte's house, because that was where the river was. But there was a house right next door to Jonte's. Old man Gren's house. It was a tumbledown old place on two floors. Old man Gren had his carpentry workshop on the ground floor and he himself lived on the top floor. Kalle wondered if it really would be possible to 'gain access' to old man Gren's house. Step right in and ask politely if they could use a window to keep an eye on something, just for a little while? Kalle knew exactly how half-baked that suggestion sounded. And there was another problem. Jonte's house and old man Gren's house were next to each other all right, but unfortunately Gren's house didn't have any windows on the top floor that faced Jonte's direction.

'I know,' said Eva-Lotta. 'We'll climb up on old Gren's roof. It's the only way.'

Kalle looked at her admiringly.

'For someone who's never read anything about criminology, you're not so stupid,' he said.

Yes, old man Gren's roof. It was the right solution. It was the perfect height for Jonte's attic window. And Jonte didn't have curtains. It would make an excellent lookout.

Feeling very happy, Kalle and Eva-Lotta went home for dinner.

5

The night was dark and quiet when the two of them came stealing through Riffraff Hill a few hours later. Utterly dark and quiet. The small wooden houses were crowded together as if competing with each other for space, and some of the heat of the scorching July day still lingered between the rows of shabby buildings. It was hot, and the whole of Riffraff Hill lay in a warm, smothering blackness. Here and there a beam of light shone out from a narrow window or from a door left open in the summer night, and the darkness was full of smells. The smell of cats, fried herrings and coffee combined with the overwhelming aroma of jasmine bushes, and the equally overwhelming aroma of someone's dustbin which should have been emptied a long time ago. Everything was still. The alleyways were deserted. The residents of Riffraff Hill didn't care to be out of doors in the evening. They had all shut themselves behind their four walls, enjoying rest and safety in their poky little kitchens, where the coffee pot bubbled away on the stove and the geraniums bloomed on the windowsills.

Anyone taking a night time stroll through Riffraff Hill wouldn't have to worry about bumping into another living thing.

'It's as silent as the grave,' said Kalle.

And he was right. Occasionally a murmur of voices could be heard coming from behind one of the lighted windows, and a dog gave a sharp bark somewhere in the distance, but quickly fell quiet. There was also someone trying to play a tune on an accordion, but they were only practising and when they stopped the silence was deeper than ever.

There was a lot more going on at Jonte's house, however. His attic window was lit up and the shrill sound of boys' voices floated out of the window. Kalle and Eva-Lotta were happy to hear that the interrogation was well under way. There was probably an exciting drama going on in there and Kalle and Eva-Lotta were determined to enjoy the performance from the front row of old man Gren's roof.

'All we have to do now is get up there,' said Eva-Lotta, cheerfully.

Yes, that was all. Kalle circled the ramshackle building to investigate the possibilities. How annoying—there was a light on in Gren's window too! Why couldn't old people sleep at night, seeing as they badly needed the rest? Then you could walk over their roofs more or less undetected. But it couldn't be helped. Detected or not, up on the roof they would go.

It turned out to be easy. Old man Gren had been thoughtful enough to prop a ladder against one of the side walls. Unfortunately, it happened to be right outside his window. The window that was lit. And the window was open behind a roller blind that was pulled down halfway. They weren't entirely sure how thrilled old man Gren would be if he suddenly stuck out his head and caught sight of two White Roses in the process of climbing up his ladder. People are rarely inclined to open their rooftops for the public to walk on. But as knights in the Wars of the Roses, they could not let themselves be put off by such a minor detail. You had to follow the call of duty regardless, even if that meant walking over old man Gren's roof.

'After you,' said Eva-Lotta encouragingly.

Slowly, slowly Kalle began climbing up the ladder. Eva-Lotta came close behind, swiftly and silently. The critical part would come when they reached the window on the top floor.

'Gren's got visitors,' Kalle whispered cautiously to Eva-Lotta. 'I can hear them talking.'

'Stick your head in and ask if we can have a biscuit,' suggested Eva-Lotta, and giggled at her own bright idea.

Kalle didn't think it was funny. He carried on up to the roof as fast as he could. Eva-Lotta became serious when it was her turn to pass the window.

It was true, Gren had visitors, that was plain to hear, but there were no biscuits on offer. Someone was standing with their back to the window, someone talking in a low voice, clearly upset. Eva-Lotta could only see part of the person, since the roller blind was half closed, but she noticed that Gren's visitor was wearing dark-green trousers. Then she heard his voice:

'Okay, okay,' he said impatiently. 'I'll try. I'll pay up. Anything to bring an end to this hell.'

Then she heard Gren's whining voice:

'You've been saying that for a long time, and I don't want to wait any longer. Surely you understand I want my money back?'

'You'll get it, I've told you.' The stranger was speaking again. 'I'll see you on Wednesday, usual place. Bring all my IOUs with you. Every blasted one. Let's put an end to this.'

'No need to be like that,' answered Gren, clearly trying to pacify him. 'Surely you understand I must have my money?'

'Bloodsucker,' said the visitor, and you could hear he meant it.

Eva-Lotta climbed on. Kalle was waiting for her, sitting on the ridge of the roof.

'There was a lot of talk about money down there,' said Eva-Lotta.

'It would have been all that percentage stuff,

I expect,' Kalle said.

'I wonder what an IOU could be?' asked Eva-Lotta thoughtfully. But then she went on hurriedly: 'Oh, never mind! Come on, Kalle!'

They had to climb right along the ridge of the roof to reach the end that faced Jonte's window. It was pretty scary balancing along the ridge in the darkness, with no stars to light their dangerous path. Nothing to hold on to, either, apart from the chimney, and that offered only temporary support once they had wobbled halfway. They weren't keen to let go of it and continue with their risky balancing act, but their courage grew at the sight of what was going on in Jonte's attic room. There was their leader, sitting on a chair, surrounded by the Red Roses who were waving their arms about and shouting at him. He merely shook his head, defiantly. Eva-Lotta and Kalle lay flat on their stomachs and prepared themselves for an enjoyable few minutes' entertainment. They could hear and see everything that was happening in there— what a triumph, what an achievement! Oh, if only their leader knew that rescue was so close! Only two metres away from him lay his two faithful followers, ready to risk life and limb for him.

There was only one small detail to be cleared up first: how would the rescue be carried out? It was all very well risking life and limb, but how would it happen across a two-metre wide gulf?

'I'm sure we'll think of something,' said Kalle, settling down as comfortably as he could in the circumstances.

Inside Jonte's room, the interrogation continued.

'Prisoner, you will be given one last chance to save your miserable life,' said Sixten, pulling Anders' arm roughly. 'Where have you hidden the Great Stonytotem?'

'You plead in vain,' Anders answered. 'For all eternity the White Roses will hold their protective hand over the Great Stonytotem. You will never find him, as sure as eggs is eggs,' he added, rather less pompously.

Kalle and Eva-Lotta nodded in silent agreement from their lookout, but Sixten, Benka and Jonte seemed genuinely angry.

'We'll have to keep him in my garage overnight, until he weakens,' said Sixten.

'Ha ha,' said Anders. 'Like Kalle and Eva-Lotta, I suppose? They escaped after five minutes, from what I heard. Exactly like I'm going to do.'

That gave the Red Roses something to think about. It was a riddle how Kalle and Eva-Lotta had managed to escape from their prison. It seemed almost supernatural. But it wouldn't be done to look impressed in front of Anders.

'Well, don't get the idea *you're* some kind of escape artist,' Sixten said. 'We'll shut you in so well you'll stay there. But first I'd like to hear some more about that language you use. Your punishment will be more lenient if you give us the key to the code.'

'Forget it,' said Anders.

'Don't be awkward,' Sixten insisted. 'You can give us a *clue* at least. You could say my name, for example. What is it in your language?'

'Tot-u-ror-non-i-pop hoh-e-a-dod,' Anders said obligingly, and he laughed sarcastically so that Sixten would understand he had been seriously insulted. He didn't dare translate it, however tempting that was, because then he would have given away the key to the Robber language. He simply laughed sarcastically again, and up on the roof opposite his comrades heartily agreed. It would have pleased their leader no end had he heard it, but for now both he and the Reds were totally unaware they had an audience.

Sixten ground his teeth in helpless rage. It was beginning to look bad for the Reds, and all that totting and popping they didn't understand was enough to drive anyone crackers. Here they were, with the Whites' leader as their captive, and they hardly knew what to do with him! He wasn't going to betray any secrets, and the noble Roses would never under any circumstances stoop so low as to use physical violence to force an admission out of him. It was true they fought mercilessly at times, until steam came out of their ears, but that was an honest tussle on a battlefield. It was out of the question to attack a helpless prisoner, three against one.

But was the prisoner really so helpless? He sat and thought about that himself. And when he had finished thinking he took a sudden dive off the chair and made a wild dash to the door in a desperate attempt to reach freedom. But it failed miserably. Within a matter of one second, three firm pairs of arms seized him and he was briskly returned to the chair.

'Nice try,' said Sixten. 'You won't get away that easily. You'll be set free when I decide, and not a minute before. And that might take a couple of years. And while we're on the subject, where have you hidden the Great Stonytotem?'

'Yes, where *have* you hidden the Great Stonytotem?' asked Jonte, and prodded Anders in the side. Instantly Anders giggled and doubled over. He was, truth be told, immensely ticklish. When Sixten saw that, a knowing smile spread across his face. He was a knight of the Red Roses and he didn't torment his prisoners. But who said you couldn't tickle them?

Tentatively he prodded Anders in the stomach. It succeeded beyond his expectations. Anders snorted like a hippopotamus and bent over double again.

That got the Red Roses going right. All together they threw themselves over their victim, and the poor Whites' leader groaned, squeaked and hiccupped with laughter.

'Where have you hidden the Great Stonytotem?' demanded Sixten, testing Anders' ribs.

'Oh... oh... oh,' panted Anders.

'Where have you hidden the Great Stonytotem?' asked Benka, tickling him mercilessly under his foot.

A convulsion of laughter was the only answer.

'Where have you hidden the Great Stonytotem?' said Jonte, and stuck his finger behind the captive's knee.

'I... give... up,' whimpered Anders. 'Out on the Prairie... a bit behind the Mansion... go along the narrow path...'

'And then what?' asked Sixten, holding up his finger in preparation.

But there was no 'then' because something totally unexpected happened. They heard a sharp crash and Jonte's room was plunged into pitch darkness. The small light bulb in the ceiling, which was the room's only source of light, had shattered into a thousand pieces.

The leader of the Whites was just as shocked as the Reds, but he regained his composure faster. Under cover of darkness he slipped like an eel through the doorway and out into the summer night. He was free.

Up on the roof opposite, Kalle reflectively stuffed his catapult back into his trouser pocket.

'I'll take some money from my piggy bank and buy Jonte a new light bulb,' he said.

Damage of another person's property was not worthy of a noble knight of the White Roses, and for Kalle it went without saying that he would replace the loss.

'But you do understand it was necessary, don't you?' he asked Eva-Lotta.

She nodded in agreement.

'It was absolutely necessary,' she said. 'Our leader was in danger. And so was the Great Stonytotem. It was definitely necessary.'

Over in Jonte's room they had managed to find a torch. In its flickering light the Reds could confirm that the prisoner had fled.

'He's a dead man!' shrieked Sixten, and rushed to the window. 'What foul scum shot out the light bulb?'

He didn't need to ask. The perpetrators stood there on the roof opposite, two thin black silhouettes, preparing for a fast retreat. They had just heard Anders' whistle and knew he was free.

Now they tore across the roof at life-threatening speed. They had to get down the ladder and reach safety before the Reds had time to meet them at the bottom. Without hesitating, they sprinted across the roof ridge in the dark, and they moved with the lightness and agility that a free and happy life had given their young, fearless, thirteen-year-old bodies.

They reached the ladder and quick as lightning began to climb down, Eva-Lotta first, Kalle right behind. They weren't thinking of Gren at this moment, but only of the Reds. Gren's window was dark. Evidently the visitor had left.

'Quick, I'm in a hurry!' whispered Kalle urgently to Eva-Lotta.

Then Gren's roller blind shot up with a bang, and the old man looked out. It came so unexpectedly and alarmed them so profoundly that Kalle suddenly lost his grip. With a loud crash he landed on the ground below, and he very nearly took Eva-Lotta with him.

'I didn't realize you were in that much of a hurry,' said Eva-Lotta. She gripped the ladder tightly so that she wouldn't fall as well, and she turned an apologetic face towards Gren. But Gren only looked with his sad, old man's eyes at Kalle on the ground, took a deep breath and said in his sad, old man's voice:

'Ah yes, the happy games of childhood. Childhood's happy, innocent games, Ah yes!'

Eva-Lotta and Kalle didn't have time to explain to Gren in detail why they were on his ladder, but then Gren didn't appear to think it was particularly surprising or unnatural. Evidently he realized that the happy, innocent games of childhood sometimes involved climbing about on ladders here and there in the neighbourhood. Kalle and Eva-Lotta said a quick goodbye and left as fast as possible, but Gren didn't seem to notice that either. He merely sighed and pulled down his roller blind.

In the dark alleyway behind Gren's house the three White Roses were reunited. They shook hands and the leader said:

'Well done, my valiant friends!'

Then they knew they had to get away quickly, because far away at the other end of the alleyway they heard a noise, and it was growing louder and louder. It was the Reds, who had finally come to their senses and were demanding revenge.

All this time the residents of Riffraff Hill had been

sleeping soundly. Now they jolted upright in their beds, half-awake and scared out of their wits. Was it the devils' horsemen passing by outside? Or if not, what in mercy's name was it? They needn't have worried, it was only the three noble knights of the Red Roses, rampaging furiously over the cobblestones. Their progress was as alarming and their cries as ear-shattering as the siren of a fire engine at its very loudest.

At first the Whites had the lead. They charged among the houses so fast their ears flapped, and they grinned smugly when they heard, far behind them, Sixten yelling dementedly about what would happen when he got hold of them. Kalle felt ecstatic as he ran in the darkness. This was the life! It was just as exciting as chasing crooks! But you could only do that in your imagination—in reality there weren't crooks, as far as he could make out—but the thudding of his pursuers' feet behind him, that was real. Anders and Eva-Lotta's panting, the uneven cobblestones under his feet, the murky, narrow alleyways and dark, tempting corners and passages and backyards where you could hide. Oh, it was marvellous, all of it! It would be an exhilarating chase. And best of all was the way his body did as he wanted it to, his feet tore along under him and breathing was easy. He felt he could speed along like this all night. He felt unbeatable, capable of outrunning a whole pack of bloodhounds, if he had to.

It occurred to him, as he ran, that it would be even more exciting if he was the only one being chased. Then he could bluff his pursuers in an entirely different way and make his manoeuvres more daring.

'Hide!' he said quickly to Anders and Eva-Lotta. 'Leave it to me. I'll be the decoy.'

Anders thought that was a sensible plan. Anything they could come up with to trick the Reds was welcome. When they had rounded the next corner Anders and Eva-Lotta darted into a dark doorway and stayed there in silence, apart from their puffing and panting.

It took a couple of seconds for the Reds to come flying round the corner. They passed so close that Anders and Eva-Lotta could have reached out and touched them. In fact, Eva-Lotta just about managed to restrain herself from grabbing a handful of Sixten's carrot-coloured mop of hair as he rushed past. But the Reds didn't notice and rushed manically on.

'As easy to fool as babies,' said Anders. 'Haven't they ever been to the cinema and seen how it's done?'

'It'll give Kalle some trouble, though,' said Eva-Lotta, listening closely to the sound of running feet fading into the darkness. 'Three nasty red foxes chasing one poor little white rabbit,' she added, suddenly filled with sympathy.

It took a while before the Reds discovered that some of their prey had evaded them, but it was too late to turn back. All they could do was carry on chasing Kalle. And no one can say they didn't try their best. Sixten sprinted like a demon, and as he ran he swore to high heaven that if Kalle managed to avoid his fate this time then he, Sixten, would walk round with a red beard as a genuine sign of sorrow and defeat. He didn't stop to think how he would get a red beard to grow on his smooth, boyish cheeks. He just kept on running.

And so did Kalle. Up and down the alleyways of Riffraff Hill, in the most deliberately convoluted twists and turns. His lead wasn't long enough to shake off his pursuers, but perhaps that isn't what he wanted. The Reds followed him, hot on his heels, and every second he enjoyed keeping them so close it felt almost dangerous.

It was quiet everywhere, but through the quiet he suddenly heard the sound of a car engine starting up. That surprised him, because cars were a rarity on Riffraff Hill. If the master detective hadn't been so involved in the Wars of the Roses, and if he hadn't had a whole pack of Red Roses on his back, it is highly likely he would have tried to catch a glimpse of that car, because you can never be too inquisitive as far as unusual occurrences are concerned. That was something he was always telling his imaginary listener. But now the master detective was on military service and so he scorched on, only slightly interested in the car, which by now had evidently driven off and was gone.

Sixten started to get impatient. He kept urging Jonte, who held the school's one hundred metre record, to try a short cut at a suitable moment and overtake Kalle, and drive him back into Sixten's clutches. That suitable moment came—a short cut appeared and Jonte took a chance that Kalle would take it. And that's how Kalle suddenly found himself face to face with Jonte, who seemed to appear out of nowhere. Kalle swung round. He didn't dare try to force his way past Jonte, because even if he had succeeded it wouldn't have taken more than a couple of seconds before Sixten and Benka came to help Jonte. No, now he had to be cunning. He found himself stuck between two evils and he had to decide what to do fast.

'We've got you!' Sixten shouted triumphantly, standing less than ten metres away. 'You're in trouble now and no mistake!'

'That's what you think,' Kalle answered, and a split second later he leapt over the fence running along one side of the alleyway. He landed in someone's dark back yard and tore across it like a shot. The Reds were right on his tail—he could hear the thuds as they jumped over the fence. But he didn't stop to listen. He was far too busy trying to work out how he could get out on to the street without having to hurdle the next fence, because whoever the owner of that fence was, he obviously didn't have a clue about the workings of the Wars of the Roses because he had topped his fence with some very nasty-looking barbed wire.

'Holy mackerel, now what do I do?' Kalle whispered to himself.

He had no time to wonder. Whatever he did, it would have to be done instantly. Quick as a flash he ducked behind a rubbish bin and crouched there, his heart pounding. There was the minutest possibility the Reds wouldn't discover him. They were right on top of him now, whispering loudly to each other, searching and searching in the darkness.

'He can't have gone over the fence,' said Jonte, 'Because he would have got stuck on the barbed wire. I know because I tried it myself once.'

'The only way out of this garden is through the hallway of that house there,' said Sixten.

'That old busybody Karlsson's hall? You want to watch out for her,' said Jonte. He knew Riffraff Hill and its residents inside out. 'That old woman's like an exploding volcano. You don't want to get on the wrong side of her.'

I wonder what's worse, thought Kalle, behind the bin. Being taken prisoner by the Reds or by that Karlsson woman? I wish I knew.

The Reds carried on looking.

'I think he's still in the back yard somewhere,' said Benka confidently. He ferreted around and finally found Kalle cowering like a dark shadow behind the rubbish bin.

His jubilant cry, even though dampened, made Sixten and Jonte leap about in excitement. It put life into Mrs Karlsson as well. She had been puzzling over the mysterious pandemonium in her back yard for quite a while, and she certainly wasn't the kind to allow mysterious pandemonium in her back yard, not if she could help it.

By now Kalle had decided that anything was better than being captured by the Red Roses, even a little disturbance of the peace in the home of Riffraff Hill's most terrifying resident. He avoided Sixten's flying fists by a millimetre and dived straight into Mrs Karlsson's hallway, hoping that would get him out on to the street. But someone came towards him in the gloom, and this someone was none other than Mrs Karlsson. She was on a mission to put an end to the rumpus, whoever was behind it, whether rats, burglars, or the King himself. Mrs Karlsson felt that she was the only person entitled to make a rumpus in this particular back yard. When Kalle came scuttling in like a terrified hare, Mrs Karlsson let him slip past her out of pure astonishment, but right behind him came Sixten, Benka and Jonte, and they ran smack into her outstretched arms. She held on to them tightly and roared like a sergeant major:

'Aha, so you're the perishers making all this ballyhoo! And in my back yard! This has gone too far. Too far, I'm telling you!'

'Sorry,' said Sixten. 'We were only—'

'*What* were you only?' shrieked Mrs Karlsson. 'What were you only—in my back yard?'

With some difficulty they managed to squirm out of her suffocating grasp.

'We were only...' stammered Sixten. 'We were... we got lost because it was so dark.'

And they rushed on without even saying goodbye.

'Try getting lost in my back yard again,' shouted Mrs Karlsson after them. 'And I'll set the police on you, so I will.'

But the Red Roses didn't hear. They were already a long way down the street. Which direction had Kalle taken? They stopped and listened, heard the light tap-tap of his footsteps in the distance and rocketed eagerly after him.

Too late Kalle realized that he had reached another dead end. This little street ended in the river—he should have remembered that. He could always throw himself into the water and swim to the other side, but that meant an awful lot of bother trying to explain his wet clothes when he got home. He wanted to try every other way out first, at least.

Fredrik the Foot, thought Kalle. Fredrik the Foot lives in this little house. He would hide me I'm sure, if I asked him.

Fredrik the Foot was the local good-natured rogue, quite harmless and a great fan of the White Roses.

In common with the town's other less savoury individuals he lived up here on Riffraff Hill, and clearly he hadn't gone to bed yet because a light was shining in his window. And there was a car parked outside. Remarkable the number of cars there were on Riffraff Hill tonight! Kalle wondered if it was the one he had heard earlier.

He had no time to wonder any more because he heard his enemies galloping down the street. He wasted no more time thinking. He opened Fredrik's door and flung himself inside.

'Evening, Fredrik,' he began, but came to a sudden stop. Fredrik wasn't alone. Fredrik was lying in his bed and beside him sat Doctor Forsberg, taking his pulse. And Doctor Forsberg, the town's doctor, was none other than Benka's dad.

'All right, Kalle?' said Fredrik, weakly. 'What do you make of me? Proper poorly and fading fast. I won't be around much longer. You should hear the racket my stomach's making.'

Under any other circumstances it would have been a pleasure for Kalle to hear the racket Fredrik's stomach was making, but not at this precise moment. Doctor Forsberg looked annoyed at the interruption, and of course Kalle understood that he wanted to be alone with Fredrik while he examined him. So there was nothing for it but to throw himself straight back into the danger on the street outside.

Kalle had underestimated the intelligence of the Reds. They had quickly worked out that he must have scooted into Fredrik the Foot's house, and they came tearing after him. Benka shot in first, well in the lead.

'You foul scum! Caught red-handed!' he yelled.

Doctor Forsberg turned round and stared straight into his son's excited face.

'Are you talking to me?' he asked.

Benka's jaw dropped in astonishment. He didn't say a word.

'Is there some kind of relay race going on through Fredriksson's sick room?' continued Doctor Forsberg. 'And how come you are out causing havoc this late at night?'

'I... I was only trying to see if you were visiting a patient,' said Benka.

'Yes, I am visiting a patient,' his father assured him. 'You have absolutely caught the foul scum red-handed. But I've finished now, so we can go home together.'

'Oh no, Dad!' shouted Benka, in utter despair.

But Doctor Forsberg slammed shut his doctor's bag and took a gentle but no-nonsense grip of Benka's hair.

'Come along, young man,' he said. 'Good night, Fredriksson! You'll be around for a while yet. I can promise you that.'

Kalle stood to one side while this conversation was going on. A smile broke out across his face and it got wider by the minute. What a drubbing for Benka! What a stonking great drubbing! Running smack into his dad! Dragged off home by his dad as if he was a little kid! And just as he was about to get his mitts on Kalle. Benka was never, ever going to live this down. 'Come along, young man'—did he need to say more?

As Benka was steered towards the door by his father's firm hand he realized the full horror of it all. He would send off a letter to the local paper: '*Must* we have parents?' Naturally, he liked his mum and dad a lot, but the way they turned up with unbelievable predictability at the most absolutely unsuitable moments could drive even the most tolerant child to despair.

Sixten and Jonte arrived panting on the street outside. Benka just had time to whisper to them 'He's in there' before he was led away to the waiting car—why, oh, why hadn't he seen it before? Sixten's and Jonte's eyes followed him, full of sympathy.

'Poor thing,' said Jonte, with a deep sigh.

Then there was no more time for sighing and sympathy. Woe to the White Roses, who were still making fools of them! Kalle would be caught, and fast.

Sixten and Jonte rushed to Fredrik the Foot's room, but there was no Kalle inside.

'There you are, Sixten. And you too, little Jonte,' Fredrik said feebly. 'You should hear the racket my stomach's making. Proper poorly and fading fast...'

'Fredrik, have you seen Kalle Blomkvist?' interrupted Sixten.

'Kalle! Yes, he was here a minute ago. He jumped out of the window,' Fredrik said, smiling wickedly.

So, the scoundrel had jumped out of the window, had he? Sure enough, both of Fredrik's windows were open, because Doctor Forsberg thought fresh air was needed. The grubby curtains that had once been white were flapping in the night breeze.

'Come on, Jonte,' shouted Sixten. 'After him! Every second counts.'

And they each raced to a window and pitched themselves out. Because every second counted.

A second later there was a splash and some angry yelling. Imagine, even Jonte, who had been born in Riffraff Hill, hadn't remembered that Fredrik's house backed directly on to the river.

'You can come out now, Kalle,' Fredrik said feebly. 'Come out and hear the racket my stomach's making.'

And Kalle climbed out of the wardrobe, absolutely delighted. He ran to the window and leaned out.

'You can swim, can't you?' he yelled. 'Or shall I go and get an inflatable boat?'

'You can just throw down your own inflated head,' Sixten yelled back furiously, and he splashed water up at Kalle's grinning face.

Kalle calmly wiped away the water and said, 'Feels

quite warm. I think you should have a nice healthy swim while you're there.'

'No, come in to me instead,' Fredrik the Foot called weakly. 'Come in, and hear the racket my stomach's making.'

'So long, I'll disappear now,' said Kalle.

'Yes, go and disappear off the face of the earth, why don't you?' said Jonte bitterly, swimming towards a little jetty close by.

The chase was over. Sixten and Jonte had to admit it.

Kalle said goodnight to Fredrik and scooted off happily to Eva-Lotta's home. In her garden was the bakery, where every day Mr Lisander baked the loaves and rolls and pastries that kept the town's residents comfortably round and content. The bakery loft was where the White Roses had their headquarters. To get there they had to clamber up a rope that dangled out of the hatch at one end of the building. There was a staircase they could have used, of course, but it was beneath the dignity of a White Rose to use such an ordinary entrance or exit, so Kalle hauled himself dutifully up the rope. When Anders and Eva-Lotta heard him, they stuck their heads eagerly out of the open hatch.

'So you got away, did you?' Anders said gleefully.

'Yes, wait till you hear,' said Kalle.

A torch spread a faint light over the headquarters, where all kinds of old furniture and junk lined the walls.

In its glow the three White Roses sat cross-legged and listened to the story of Kalle's marvellous escape.

'Well done, oh valiant warrior,' said Anders, when Kalle had finished.

'Yes, and considering it's only the first day of battle I think the White Roses have done brilliantly well,' said Eva-Lotta.

Then they heard a woman's voice cutting through the silence outside.

'Eva-Lotta! If you don't come in this instant and get to bed, I'll send your father up to fetch you!'

'All right Mum, I'm coming!' shouted Eva-Lotta.

Her faithful companions stood up to leave.

'Bye, see you tomorrow,' said Eva-Lotta. Then she laughed happily.

'Ha ha! So the Reds thought they could get the Great Stonytotem, did they? Ha ha!'

'But they got a nasty shock instead,' said Kalle.

'But see, that very night they were sent away empty-handed,' said Anders, making a dignified exit down the rope.

7

Can there be anywhere in the world more placid and uneventful than this little town? thought Mrs Lisander. But how could anything happen anyway, in this heat?

She sauntered between the stalls in the square, absent-mindedly choosing from the goods that were on display. It was market day and lots of people were out in the square and surrounding streets, and although the whole town ought to be bubbling with life and movement, it wasn't. Not at all. It was sleepy, the same as usual. The water in the fountain in front of the town hall spouted sleepily from the jaws of the bronze lions, and the bronze lions were looking rather sleepy as well.

The music coming from the café gardens down by the riverside was slow and drowsy, a kind of last waltz slap bang in the middle of the morning. The sparrows pecking at the fallen crumbs between the tables made half-hearted hops from time to time, but in fact they looked half asleep as well.

Everything's half asleep, thought Mrs Lisander.

People scarcely had the energy to move. They stood in groups in the square, chatting about this and that, and if they had to walk a few steps they did it slowly and very reluctantly. The heat was to blame, of course.

It really was very hot, this last day in the month of July. Mrs Lisander would always remember it as one of the hottest days she had ever known. In fact, the whole month had been dry and sweltering, and today it seemed as if July had made up its mind to break its own record before time ran out.

'Feels like thunder,' people said to each other. Many of them who lived in the surrounding countryside and had come to the market by horse and cart decided to go home earlier than usual. They didn't want to risk being caught in a storm.

Mrs Lisander bought a large punnet of cherries from a farmer who was in a hurry to leave and was selling them at a knock-down price. She put them in her shopping bag, very satisfied with her bargain. She was about to walk on when Eva-Lotta popped up out of nowhere and blocked her path.

At last, someone who doesn't look half asleep, thought Mrs Lisander. She looked at her daughter lovingly, taking in every detail: the happy face, the alert blue eyes, the rumpled blonde hair and the long suntanned legs sticking out from under a light, freshly-ironed summer dress.

'I just saw you buy some cherries,' Eva-Lotta said. 'I don't suppose I can take a fistful, by any chance?'

'Of course. Help yourself,' her mother said. She held out the bag and Eva-Lotta grabbed a handful of the plump red fruit.

'Where are you off to, by the way?' asked Mrs Lisander.

'Nothing you need to know about,' said Eva-Lotta, and spat out a cherry stone. 'Secret mission. Incredibly secret mission!'

'I see. Well just make sure you're not late home for dinner.'

'What do you take me for?' said Eva-Lotta. 'I've never, ever been late for any meal since the time I missed my bottle on my Christening day.'

Mrs Lisander smiled at her.

'I love you,' she said.

Eva-Lotta nodded in answer to this undeniable fact and carried on across the square, leaving a trail of cherry stones behind her.

Her mother stood there for a moment, watching her leave. And all of a sudden she had a sense of impending doom. Oh Lord, how fragile that girl looked! So young and vulnerable. It wasn't that long since she was eating baby porridge, and now here she was, chattering on about 'secret missions'. Was that all right? Should she be taking more care of her daughter?

Mrs Lisander sighed and walked slowly away.

She felt the heat would soon drive her mad, and in that case it was better to be in the safe surroundings of her own home.

Eva-Lotta wasn't at all bothered by the heat. She enjoyed it, just as she enjoyed the jostle of people on the streets and the juice of the fruit as it ran down her chin. It was market day, and she liked market days. She liked most days, if she stopped to think about it, except the ones when they had sewing lessons at school. But now it was the summer holidays.

She wandered across the square and carried on down Lillgatan, past the café garden and on to the bridge over the river. To tell the truth, she really didn't want to leave the activity behind her, but she had a secret mission to carry out. It so happened that the leader of the Whites had ordered her to fetch the Great Stonytotem and take it to a safer hiding place. During his painful interrogation Anders had almost revealed its hiding place, and you could bet your life that ever since then the Reds had been combing every single square millimetre along the narrow path behind the Mansion. But seeing as they hadn't had to put up with any victorious bragging from the Reds, she was pretty certain the Great Stonytotem was still where the Whites had put it—on top of a large rock right beside the path. It lay there fully visible in a small hollow in the rock. It was actually ridiculously easy to find, Anders said. It was only a question of time before the Reds would lay their hands on the precious trophy. But today was market day and it was highly likely Sixten and Jonte wouldn't be able to tear themselves away from the carousel and shooting range at the fairground behind the train station. Today was Eva-Lotta's chance to take the Great Stonytotem from its currently insecure hiding place without being seen. Her leader had also decided where its new hiding place was going to be: in the castle ruins, beside the water pump in the courtyard. That meant Eva-Lotta, in the oppressive, thundery heat, had to trudge all the way over the Prairie, then all the way back again to other side of the town, and after that climb the steep path up to the ruins, which lay high up overlooking the town in completely the opposite direction from the Mansion. Honestly, you had to be a most devoted knight of the Red Roses to undertake such a mission without complaining. But Eva-Lotta was devoted. You might think it wouldn't have mattered if she had taken the Great Stonytotem and put it in her pocket, at least until the weather was a bit cooler. But if you thought that it means you don't understand the slightest thing about Great Stonytotems, or the wars between the Reds and the Whites.

And why exactly was Eva-Lotta the one who had been entrusted with the mission? Couldn't the leader have sent Kalle? No, because a clueless father had made Kalle his errand boy and extra assistant in his grocery shop today, when the country people came into town to stock up on sugar and coffee and salted herrings. Couldn't the leader have gone himself? No, because the leader had to keep an eye on his own father's shop. Mr Bengtsson the shoemaker didn't like working on market days, or any other special days come to that. On those occasions he took time off to join in the festivities. But that was no reason for him to shut his workshop. Someone might come in to collect a pair of shoes, or leave some for repair, even though it was market day. That was why he swore he'd teach his son a lesson or two if he so much as set foot outside the workshop.

Eva-Lotta, devoted knight of the White Roses, is the one who has been entrusted with the task, the secret and sacred task of carrying the mighty Great Stonytotem from one safe hiding place to another. This isn't just any old task, it is a ritual, a mission. What does it matter if the sun is blazing down red-hot over the Prairie, and black clouds are piling up on the horizon? What does it matter if you can't join in the fun of market day, that you must leave the centre where everything's happening? Because that's exactly what Eva-Lotta did when she turned off over the bridge and followed the road out towards the Prairie.

But had she really done that? No, the place where it's all happening isn't necessarily in the middle of a busy market. On this particular day the place where it was all happening was somewhere else entirely.

And at this very minute, on her bare suntanned legs, Eva-Lotta was walking straight into it.

Those clouds were starting to look really menacing. Blue-black, nasty, enough to make you feel quite anxious. Eva-Lotta walks slowly, because out here on the Prairie it is so hot the air is practically quivering.

Phew, the Prairie is so huge it takes forever to walk across it! But Eva-Lotta isn't the only one out there, walking in the sunshine. It almost makes her happy when she sees, way ahead of her, old man Gren. It's him without a doubt, no one else totters like that when they walk. And Gren is also on his way to the Mansion, by the look of things.

Yes, look, he turns off on to that narrow path between the hazel bushes and disappears from Eva-Lotta's sight. Jumping Jehoshaphat, he's not after the Great Stonytotem as well, is he? Eva-Lotta grins to herself at the thought of it. But soon she stops and squints through the hazy sunshine. Someone else is coming from the other direction, someone not from town, clearly, because he has come from the road which winds out into the countryside after passing the Mansion. Well, if it isn't that bloke with the green trousers! Yes, of course, it's Wednesday today, the day he was going to get back his

IOUs, or whatever they were called. Eva-Lotta wonders what happens when you get your IOUs back. All that percentages lark—it must be enormously complicated. And honestly, what a lot of bunkum grown-ups got involved in. 'See you on Wednesday, usual place,' Green Trousers had said. So, that was out here, was it? But did it *have* to be right next to the Great Stonytotem? Were there *no* other bushes where they could meet and do their percentaging? No, evidently not. And now Green Trousers has swung on to the path between the hazel bushes too.

Eva-Lotta walks even slower. She's in no particular hurry, and it would be best if that bloke got his IOUs back in peace and quiet, before she collects the Great Stonytotem. She goes into the Mansion while she's waiting, and investigates the small passages and cubbyholes. The Mansion might become a battleground again soon, so it would be smart to know your way around in there.

She looks out through one of the windows at the back. Oh dear, the whole sky has gone dark. The sun has vanished and there is an ominous sound of thunder in the distance. She must hurry. She must collect the Great Stonytotem and get out of here! And she runs out through the door, runs as fast as she can, runs to the path between the hazel bushes, all the time hearing the rumbling thunder. She runs on, runs... oh, now she stops. She has collided headlong with someone who has been walking along the path from the opposite direction, and he is in just as much a hurry as she is. At first she sees only the green trousers and the white shirt, but then she lifts her head and sees his face. Help, what a face! So pale, so nervous—can a grown man really be that afraid of thunder? Eva-Lotta almost feels sympathy for him.

But it seems he isn't the slightest bit interested in her. He gives her a rapid glance, looking scared and angry at the same time, and hurries to get past her on the narrow path.

Eva-Lotta doesn't like people looking at her like that, as if she was something unpleasant. She is used to people's faces lighting up when they see her. And she doesn't want that bloke to disappear until she has pointed out that she is a perfectly friendly individual and would like to be treated as one.

'Excuse me, could you tell me what the time is?' she says politely, simply to say something, and to show him that, well, that they are civilised human beings, even if they have happened to bump into each other among the bushes.

The man jerks to a stop, unwillingly. At first he looks as if he isn't going to answer her question, but finally he looks at his watch and mumbles:

'Quarter to two.'

Then off he rushes. Eva-Lotta watches him go. She can

see a bundle of papers sticking out of one of his trouser pockets. One of his green trouser pockets.

And then he's gone. But there, lying on the path, is a crumpled piece of white paper. He dropped it in his hurry.

Eva-Lotta picks it up and looks at it curiously. 'IOU' it says at the top. Oh, so that's what an IOU looks like. I ask you! Is this anything to make such a fuss about?

Then there is a crack, an ear-splitting crack, and Eva-Lotta jumps in fear. It isn't that she's scared of thunder, but now, at this very moment, out here on the Prairie, it feels so eerie all of a sudden. It's very dark here among the bushes. And there is something awful and menacing in the air. Oh, if only she was at home! She must hurry, she must absolutely hurry.

But first the Great Stonytotem! A knight of the White Roses does her duty, even with her heart in her mouth. Only a few steps left to that rock. Just through those bushes over there. Eva-Lotta runs...

First all she can do is whimper. She doesn't move a muscle. She sees and she whimpers. Perhaps... oh, perhaps she is only dreaming! Perhaps there really isn't something lying there... something slumped beside the rock...

She covers her face with her hands, spins round and runs, and weird, terrible sounds come up from her throat.

She runs, even though her legs are shaking beneath her. She doesn't hear the claps of thunder or feel the rain drenching her, she doesn't feel the hazel branches whipping against her face. She runs the way you do in dreams, when you are being chased by unknown terrors.

Over the Prairie. Over the bridge. The familiar streets are suddenly empty and abandoned in the pouring rain.

Home! Home! Finally! She flings open the garden gate. There in the bakery is her dad. He is standing there with his baking trays, wearing his white baker's clothes. He is large and safe as usual, and you get covered in flour if you get anywhere near him. Dad is the same as usual, even if the world is terrible and changed and impossible to live in any longer. Eva-Lotta throws herself frantically into his arms, holds herself close, wraps her arms around his neck, tight, tight. Buries her tear-stained face into his shoulder and sobs quietly:

'Dad! Help me! Old man Gren...'

'My child, what about old man Gren?'

And even more quietly, with even more sobbing:

'He's lying dead out on the Prairie.'

Was this the town that was so sleepy and tranquil and quiet?

Not any more. Within an hour everything changed. The whole town buzzed like a beehive, police cars came and went, telephones rang, people talked and made wild guesses, were shocked and bewildered, and asked Constable Björk if it was true that the culprit had already been caught. They shook their heads and said: 'To think old Gren would come to such a bad end... oh, dear... well, we had an idea what he was up to, so perhaps it's not unexpected... but still... heaven forbid, how dreadful!' And hordes of curious people streamed out to the Prairie.

The whole area surrounding the Mansion was cordoned off and guarded by the police, so people couldn't get anywhere near it. With startling speed, officers from police headquarters in Stockholm had arrived with their own team. A search of the crime scene was underway, everything was being photographed, every inch of the ground searched and every piece of information logged. Had the murderer left any clues? Footprints, that kind of thing? No, nothing! And if there had been any, the heavy rain would have destroyed them. There was nothing, not so much as a discarded cigarette end, to lead them to the murderer. The forensics expert who examined the body could confirm that Gren had been killed by a shot from behind. The old man's wallet and watch hadn't been taken. It didn't appear to be a robbery.

The chief inspector had wanted to interview the young girl who had made the hideous discovery, but Doctor Forsberg wouldn't allow it. The girl was in shock and must be left in peace. The Chief Inspector had to accept that, but he was concerned about the delay. Doctor Forsberg had been able to tell him that the girl had cried and said repeatedly: 'He was wearing green trousers!' Clearly she meant the murderer.

But you couldn't issue a description over the whole country that consisted only of a pair of green trousers. If it really was the murderer the girl had seen, and the Chief Inspector wasn't entirely certain about that, then by this time he would have changed out of his green trousers and put on something else. But despite that, and to be on the safe side, the chief inspector had contacted every police authority in the country and asked them to keep a lookout for pairs of green trousers which could in any way be suspicious. Apart from that, all they could do was follow every imaginable routine procedure until the girl had recovered enough to be interviewed properly.

Eva-Lotta was lying in her mum's bed, the safest place she knew. Doctor Forsberg had visited her, and she had been given some tablets to help her sleep without having nightmares. And her mum and dad had promised to sit beside her all through the night.

But even so, stubborn thoughts chased each other around her brain. Oh, if only she hadn't gone to the Mansion! Now everything was ruined. Nothing would ever, ever be any fun again. How could there be any fun, when people could treat each other so badly? She had known things like this could happen, but she hadn't known the way she did now. And to think of how she and Anders had teased Kalle, and talked about 'murderers' as if it was something hilarious, something to joke about! It was unbearable to remember that now. She would never do it again. You shouldn't say things like that even as a joke, because then somehow you might summon up the evil and make it happen in reality. And what if it was her fault that Gren... that Gren... no, she didn't want to think about it. But she would change, yes, she would! She would become more ladylike, as Constable Björk had said. She would never take part in the Wars of the Roses again, because wasn't it precisely the Wars of the Roses that had got her mixed up in all this... this thing she mustn't think about, if she didn't want her head to explode.

No, this would be the end of the fighting as far as she was concerned. She wouldn't play again, ever! Oh, how bored she would be!

Tears filled her eyes again, and she grasped her mum's hand.

'Mum, I feel so old,' she sobbed. 'I feel like I'm almost fifteen.'

Then she fell asleep. But before she sank into merciful oblivion she wondered what Kalle was thinking. Kalle, who had been hunting for murderers for years! What was he doing, now that one really had turned up?

Master Detective Blomkvist heard the news as he was standing behind the counter in his dad's shop, in the middle of wrapping two salted herrings in newspaper for a customer. It was precisely then that Mrs Karlsson from Riffraff Hill came barging in through the door, bursting with the news and the need to stir up a little sensationalism. Within two minutes the entire shop was seething with questions and shouting and horrified shuddering. Business came to a standstill as the customers flocked around Mrs Karlsson. She ranted and blustered and her saliva sprayed everywhere. She couldn't wait to tell them everything she had heard, and more besides.

Master Detective Blomkvist, the person who should have been responsible for keeping the town safe, stood at the counter, listening. He said nothing. He asked nothing. He was totally paralysed. When he had heard most of it he slunk unnoticed into the storeroom and flopped down on an empty sugar crate.

He sat there for a long time. Did he by any chance have a chat with his invisible listener? Wouldn't this have been the perfect time? No, he didn't. He kept quiet, but he was thinking a few things.

Kalle Blomkvist, he thought, you are a prize duffer, that's what you are! Master Detective, my foot! The most horrendous crimes can take place under our very noses and you stand calmly behind the counter wrapping fish. Carry on with that, why don't you? At least it means you're good for *something*!

He sat there with his head in his hands, his thoughts whirling. Oh, why did he have to be serving in the shop today of all days? Otherwise Anders would have sent him and not Eva-Lotta. And then he would have been the one to discover the body. Or who knows—perhaps he could have come in time to stop it happening, and seen the perpetrator severely reprimanded and locked up behind bars. Like he usually did.

But with a sigh he reminded himself that he only did that in his imagination. And finally Kalle really understood what had happened. He understood it, his blood ran cold, and all at once he had no desire to be a master detective ever again. This was no pretend murder that you solved elegantly and then boasted about to an invisible listener. It was an appalling, vile, disgusting reality that almost made him want to be sick. He despised himself for it but in fact he was glad he hadn't gone today instead of Eva-Lotta. Poor Eva-Lotta!

Without asking permission, he left the shop. He felt he had to go and talk to Anders. Trying to talk to Eva-Lotta wouldn't get him anywhere, he realized, because Mrs Karlsson had blabbed and said 'the baker's girl is terrible overcome, doctor's with her now'—so the whole town must know.

But Anders didn't know. He was sitting in the shoemaker's workshop, reading *Treasure Island*. No one had been in since early morning, and that was lucky because Anders was on an island in the South Seas, surrounded by marauding pirates, and wasn't the faintest bit interested in shoes that needed new soles or heels. When Kalle suddenly flung open the door Anders stared at him, half expecting to see Long John Silver hobbling towards him. He was hugely relieved to see it was only Kalle. He shot up from his stool and sang loudly:

'Fifteen men on a dead man's chest,
Yo ho ho and a bottle of rum'

Kalle shivered.

'Shut up,' he said, 'Shut up!'

'That's what our singing teacher says, too, as soon as I sing a note,' Anders admitted happily.

Kalle looked as if he was about to say something, but Anders got in first.

'Any idea whether Eva-Lotta has collected the Great Stonytotem yet?'

Kalle looked at him disapprovingly. How much guff was Anders going to spew out before Kalle could bring himself to say anything? He tried again, but Anders interrupted him this time as well. He had been sitting quietly for so long that he was desperate to talk. He picked up *Treasure Island* and waved it under Kalle's nose.

'What a cracking book!' he said. 'It's so exciting, you wouldn't believe it. We should have lived then, Kalle. What an adventure! Nothing happens these days.'

'Doesn't it?' said Kalle. 'You don't know what you're talking about.'

And he told Anders what was happening these days. Anders' dark eyes grew even darker when he heard about the trouble his orders to move the Great Stonytotem had caused. He wanted to rush off to Eva-Lotta straight away, and if not exactly comfort her then at least show her he thought he was an absolute rat to have sent her on that mission.

'But how was I to know there would be people lying about stone dead all over the place?' he said to Kalle, dejectedly.

Kalle sat opposite him, distractedly hammering a row of nails into the shoemaker's bench.

'No, how could you know?' he said. 'You don't come across them that often.'

'Come across what?'

'Dead people, at the Mansion.'

'No, exactly,' said Anders. 'And by the way, Eva-Lotta can handle it, no question. Any other girl would go completely doolally, but not her. She'll give the police tons of leads, you see if she doesn't.'

Kalle nodded.

'Maybe she saw someone who... who could have done it.'

Anders shuddered, but he wasn't nearly as affected as Kalle. He was a cheerful, optimistic and very active boy, and unusual events made him want to do something about it, even if the events were terrifying. He wanted to do something now—leap in and get started on their detective work and catch the killer, preferably within the space of one hour. He wasn't a dreamer like Kalle. It would be wrong to say that Kalle, despite his daydreaming, wasn't active too—there were people who could confirm that, to their cost—but the way Kalle worked was different. He always began by taking his time to think things through. He came up with some staggeringly clever things at times, but often it was nothing more than his imagination running wild.

Anders didn't waste time imagining. His body was so fizzing with energy that he found it agonising to sit still for any length of time. It wasn't chance that had made him the leader of the White Roses. He was the obvious choice: good-natured and talkative and inventive, and always ready to take the lead, whatever the circumstances. That was Anders. A more fragile character would have been damaged by the situation at home, where his father was an intolerable tyrant. But not Anders. He kept out of the way as much as he could, and he didn't take his father's rages to heart. The aggression ran off him like water off a duck's back, and five minutes after the worst outburst Anders was out of doors and running about again, as happy as ever.

It was unthinkable that he should be sitting here on his backside when there were other, more important things demanding his intervention.

'Come on, Kalle. I'll shut the workshop. Dad can say what he likes.'

'Do you really dare?' asked Kalle, who knew all about the shoemaker.

'No problem,' said Anders.

Of course he dared. First, all he had to do was explain to customers why the shoemaker's workshop was closed right in the middle of a working day. He picked up a pen and wrote on a piece of paper:

CLOSED DUE TO MURDER

Then he tacked it to the outside of the door and turned the key.

'Have you gone raving mad?' said Kalle, when he read it. 'You can't write that.'

'Can't I?' said Anders. He put his head on one side and considered. Maybe Kalle was right, perhaps the note could be misunderstood. He tore it down, ran inside and wrote another one. Then he tacked it to the door and walked quickly away. Kalle followed his leader.

Mrs Magnusson from across the road arrived shortly afterwards to pick up a pair of shoes that had been left for repair. Wide-eyed in astonishment she read the note:

In consideration of the congenial
weather this workshop is staying
CLOSED

Mrs Magnusson shook her head. He had never been the sharpest tool in the box, that shoemaker, but now he had completely lost his wits. The congenial weather! Have you ever heard anything like it!

Anders hurried towards the Prairie. Kalle followed, extremely reluctantly. It was the last place he wanted to go, but Anders was convinced the police were waiting for

Kalle's help. Admittedly, in the past he had teased the master detective about his obsession, but he forgot that now, when a genuine crime had actually been committed. All he could think of was Kalle's amazing work last year. It was only thanks to Kalle that those jewellery thieves had been caught. Yes, Kalle was a first-class detective, and Anders admitted his superiority willingly. He was convinced the police hadn't forgotten, either.

'You know they'll be pleased when you offer them your services,' he said. 'You'll solve this in no time. I can be your assistant.'

Kalle was in a fix. He couldn't bring himself to explain to Anders that it was only pretend murders he could handle, and that he thought it was nothing short of horrendous having to deal with a real murder. He dragged his feet as he walked, and that made Anders impatient.

'Hurry up,' he said. 'Every second counts at a time like this. You should know that better than anyone.'

'I think we'll let the police take care of it themselves,' Kalle said, trying to get off the hook.

'How can you say that?' said Anders, aghast. 'You know more than anyone how they can make an absolute dog's dinner of everything. You've said so yourself, many times. Don't be a dope, and come here!'

He grabbed the reluctant detective by the arm, forcing him to walk beside him.

Eventually they reached the cordoned-off area.

'Kalle,' said Anders. 'Have you thought of something?'

'No, what?' Kalle said.

'The Great Stonytotem is out of reach. If the Reds want it, they'll have to break through the police barrier.'

Kalle nodded thoughtfully. Many fates had befallen the Great Stonytotem, but this was the first time it had been guarded by police.

Constable Björk was patrolling the protected area and Anders made a beeline towards him. He dragged Kalle along and delivered him at Constable Björk's feet, rather like a dog that drags an object to its owner and sits there waiting for praise.

'Constable Björk, here's Kalle,' he said, expectantly.

'So I see,' said Constable Björk. 'And what does Kalle want?'

'Let him through, so he can start investigating the crime scene,' said Anders.

But Constable Björk shook his head and looked deadly serious.

'Hop it, lads,' he said. 'Go home! And be glad you're too young to understand what's happened!'

Kalle's face reddened. He understood very well. He understood without a doubt that this was no place for Master Detective Blomkvist, with his chiselled features and big words. If only he could get Anders to understand that as well!

'Typical,' said Anders crossly, as they turned to walk

back to town. 'Even if you had solved every murder since Cain killed Abel the police would never admit that a private detective is any good.'

Kalle squirmed uncomfortably. He had said more or less the same thing to himself many times. He was hoping like mad that Anders would change the subject. But Anders went on:

'They'll get stuck sooner or later, of course. But promise me you won't take on the case until they come begging to you on their bare knees.'

Kalle promised readily.

Small, silent groups of people were standing everywhere. They were staring intently at those bushes, where a team of experts was at this very minute trying to find the answer to a drama that had cost someone his life. It was weirdly still on the Prairie today. Kalle felt miserable, and even Anders was starting to be affected by the depressing atmosphere. Maybe Constable Björk was right. This was nothing for Kalle to get involved in, however skilful a detective he was.

They wandered glumly home.

Sixten, Benka and Jonte were also on their way home from the Prairie. They had taken a day off from fighting the Wars of the Roses, just as Anders had reckoned, and they had spent many happy hours riding on the carousel and shooting at targets down at the fair.

But a short while ago the shocking news had reached

the fairground, and customers quickly melted away. Sixten, Benka and Jonte had also raced out to the Prairie—only to realize they might as well go home. And just as they reached that conclusion, they bumped into Anders and Kalle.

No warrior-like words were exchanged between the Reds and the Whites today. As one group they traipsed back to town, all five of them, and while they were walking they thought about death more than they had ever done before in their young lives.

They felt enormous sympathy for Eva-Lotta.

'I feel sorry for her, actually,' said Sixten. 'They say she's feeling really ropey, lying there and crying all the time.'

Anders felt more upset by this than by the whole nasty business itself. He gulped a couple of times. It was his fault Eva-Lotta was lying there, crying.

'Perhaps we ought to do something,' he said at last. 'Take her some flowers, or something.'

The other four stared at him as if they couldn't believe their ears. Take flowers to a girl? He must be convinced Eva-Lotta was on her last legs!

But the more they thought about it, the more considerate it seemed. Eva-Lotta would have some flowers. She honestly deserved it. Deeply moved, Sixten went home and stole one of his mum's red geraniums, and carrying the pot between them all five marched towards the baker's house.

Eva-Lotta was sleeping and wasn't to be disturbed. But her mum accepted the geranium and put it on Eva-Lotta's bedside table, so she would see it as soon as she woke up.

That wasn't the last present Eva-Lotta would get for her part in the drama.

9

They sat on the veranda and waited, the friendly chief inspector, Constable Björk, and one other person. It was important that the little girl didn't feel anxious about the interview, said the chief inspector. No more anxious than she was feeling at the moment, that is. That's why it was good that Constable Björk was there, because he belonged to the local police force and knew the girl. And so that the interview would have the feeling of an ordinary little chat, it was going to be held here in the girl's home, on the sunny veranda, and not at the police station. Children get worried in unfamiliar surroundings, said the chief inspector. And the girl's testimony was going to be recorded, so she wouldn't have to be bothered more than once. After she had told them everything she knew, she could forget it all. Forget that there was such evil in the world. Said the chief inspector.

And now they were sitting on the veranda, waiting for her to appear. It was early in the morning and she wasn't up and dressed yet. While they waited, Mrs Lisander offered them coffee and freshly baked Danish pastries, and they certainly needed it. Those poor policemen had worked almost all night and hadn't had any food or sleep.

It was a wonderful morning. The air was fresh and clear after yesterday's thunderstorm, the roses and peonies in the baker's garden looked newly-washed, and chaffinches and blackbirds twittered cheerfully in the old apple tree. It all felt very welcoming and safe. You would hardly believe that the three people eating and drinking were on-duty police officers in the middle of a murder investigation. On a lovely summer morning like this, you really didn't want to think that things like that existed.

The chief inspector took a third Danish pastry and said:

'To tell you the truth, I doubt we'll get much out of the girl—Eva-Lotta, isn't it? I don't think her testimony will make much difference to the investigation. Children can't make objective observations. They have such vivid imaginations.'

'Eva-Lotta is very matter-of-fact,' said Constable Björk.

Mr Lisander the baker came out on to the veranda. He had a wrinkle in his forehead where normally there wasn't one. That wrinkle meant he was worried about his beloved only daughter, and he was unhappy because he had to let these police officers torment her with their questions.

'She's coming now,' he said abruptly. 'Can I be present during the interview?'

After a short hesitation the chief inspector agreed, on the condition he kept completely quiet and didn't interfere in the interview in any way.

'Well, I suppose Eva-Lotta might as well have her father with her,' said the chief inspector. 'It'll make her feel safer. It's possible she's feeling a little afraid of me.'

'Why would I feel that?' said a calm voice from the doorway, and Eva-Lotta stepped out into the sunshine. She looked at the chief inspector with a serious expression. Why would she feel afraid of him? Eva-Lotta wasn't afraid of people. In her experience most of them were kind and friendly and wouldn't do you any harm. It was only yesterday she had discovered how wicked some people could be. But she didn't see any reason to include the chief inspector among them. She knew he was sitting there because he had to. She knew she had to tell him everything about the ghastly thing that had happened on the Prairie, and she was prepared to do that. So why should she be afraid?

Her head felt muzzy after all the crying and because she had slept so deeply. She wasn't happy, but she was calm, completely calm.

'Good morning, little Lisa-Lotta,' said the chief inspector.

'Eva-Lotta,' said Eva-Lotta. 'Morning!'

'Eva-Lotta, of course. Come and sit here, Eva-Lotta, and you and I will have a little chat. It won't take long, and then you can go and play with your dolls again.'

This is what he said to Eva-Lotta, who was feeling fifteen years old!

'I stopped playing with dolls ten years ago,' Eva-Lotta informed him.

Constable Björk was right—this really was a matter-of-fact young lady! The chief inspector realized he would have to change his tone and speak to Eva-Lotta as if she were an adult.

'Tell me everything now,' he said. 'You were out at the mur... out on the Prairie yesterday afternoon, am I right? Why did you go there on your own?'

Eva-Lotta clamped her mouth shut. Then she said:

'I... I can't tell you. It's a secret. I was out on a secret mission.'

'Listen, Eva-Lotta,' said the chief inspector.' We are trying to investigate a murder. There can be no secrets here. What were you doing out at the Mansion yesterday?'

'I was going to get the Great Stonytotem,' Eva-Lotta said reluctantly.

A rather long explanation was needed before the inspector was clear about what a Great Stonytotem actually was. In his police report, made after the interview, all he wrote was: *'Explaining her movements, Lisander said that on the afternoon of 28 July she set off to the area of common land west of town with the intention of collecting a so-called Great Stonytotem.'*

'Did you see any people while you were there?' asked the chief inspector, after the mystery with the Great Stonytotem had been cleared up.

'Yes,' said Eva-Lotta. 'I... I saw Gren and one other person.'

The chief inspector brightened up.

'Tell me exactly how and where you saw him,' he said.

Eva-Lotta told him how she had seen Gren from behind, about a hundred metres away...'

'Stop there,' said the chief inspector. 'How could you know it was Gren from such a distance?'

'I can tell the inspector doesn't come from this town,' said Eva-Lotta. 'Every single person round here would have recognized Gren from his walk. Aren't I right, Constable Björk?'

Björk confirmed that she was.

Eva-Lotta went on with her explanation about how she had seen Gren turn off along the narrow path and disappear among the bushes, and how the man with dark-green trousers had appeared from the other direction and gone the same way as Gren.

'Have you any idea what the time was?' asked the chief inspector, even though he knew children hardly ever gave the right time.

'Half past one.'

'How do you know that? Did you look at your watch?'

'No,' said Eva-Lotta, turning pale. 'But I asked the mur... the murderer about fifteen minutes later.'

The chief inspector looked at his colleagues. Had they ever heard anything like it? Clearly, this interview was going to provide more answers than he had imagined.

He leaned forward and stared directly into Eva-Lotta's eyes.

'You asked the murderer, you say. Are you telling us you know who Gren's murderer was? Perhaps you saw it happen?'

'No,' said Eva-Lotta. 'But when I see someone vanish into a load of bushes and then a second persons dives in after him, and a few minutes later I find the first person dead, I can't help suspecting the second person. Gren could have fallen over and banged his head, of course, but I'd like proof of that first.'

Björk was right, this child was very matter-of-fact.

She went on to say that when she saw the two men go down the path leading to the Great Stonytotem's hiding place, she had gone into the Mansion to pass the time, and had stayed there for fifteen minutes at the most.

'What happened next?' asked the chief inspector.

Eva-Lotta's face clouded over. The next bit would be difficult.

'I ran into him on the path,' she said softly. 'I asked him what the time was, and he said a quarter to two.'

The chief inspector looked very satisfied. Forensics had been able to establish that the murder took place sometime between twelve and three, but this girl's evidence made it possible to be more precise: between half past one and a quarter to two. Such a thing could be significant. Eva-Lotta truly was an invaluable witness!

He went on with his questioning.

'What did the man look like? Tell me everything you remember! All the details.'

Eva-Lotta described the dark-green trousers, white shirt, dark red tie, wristwatch. The black hair on the back of his hands.

'What was his face like?' asked the chief inspector eagerly.

'He had a moustache,' said Eva-Lotta. 'And longish, dark hair that flopped over his forehead. Not that old, and quite nice-looking, but afraid and angry, too. He ran away from me as fast as he could. He was in such a hurry that he dropped an IOU, and he didn't notice.'

The chief inspector took a deep breath.

'What in heaven's name did you say? He dropped an IOU?'

'An IOU,' said Eva-Lotta importantly. 'Don't you know what that is, Chief Inspector? It's just a piece of paper with 'IOU' written at the top. I can assure you it's nothing other than a piece of paper, but people make an awful lot of fuss about IOUs, believe me.'

The chief inspector looked at his colleagues again. The questioning among the old man's neighbours over on Riffraff Hill yesterday had made it perfectly clear that Gren ran a little money-lending business on the side. Many of them had noticed that he had mysterious visitors at night, although not all that often. Clearly he preferred to meet his clients in various places on the outskirts of town. During a search at his home, a great many IOUs in different names had been found. Every name had been logged and the police were preparing to trace every single one of Gren's mysterious customers. One of them could be the murderer. The chief inspector had been confident all along that the murder had taken place precisely because the person concerned wanted to get himself out of the spiral of debt he was tangled up in. That was the obvious motive for the crime. And you don't do a thing like that unless you are sure you can get hold of every document that could connect you to the crime.

And here was the girl, telling him that the murderer had dropped an IOU the bushes. An IOU with his name on. The chief inspector was so eager that his voice shook as he leaned towards Eva-Lotta.

'Did you pick up that IOU?'

'I did,' said Eva-Lotta.

'What did you do with it?' asked the chief inspector, holding his breath.

Eva-Lotta considered the question. There was dead silence while she was thinking. All that could be heard was the chaffinch twittering in the apple tree.

'I don't remember,' said Eva-Lotta.

The chief inspector gave a long, drawn-out groan.

'Honestly, it was only a little piece of paper,' said Eva-Lotta, to comfort him.

Then the chief inspector picked up her hand and explained to her very carefully that an IOU is quite an important document stating that a person has borrowed money from someone else and agrees to pay it back later. You confirm this with your signature. The man who killed Gren obviously did it because he had no money to pay his debts. He had shot a man in cold blood so that he could get back his IOUs, which Eva-Lotta thought were so trivial. And his name must have been written on the piece of paper he dropped on the path. Did Eva-Lotta understand now that it was absolutely vital she remembered what she had done with the IOU?

Eva-Lotta understood, and she tried, she really did. She remembered standing with the IOU in her hand. She remembered that there was a deafening clap of thunder at that moment. But after that she remembered nothing—well yes, the awful thing that happened immediately afterwards. But she couldn't recall anything else at all about the IOU. Dismayed, she explained this to the chief inspector.

'I don't suppose you read the name on the IOU?' the chief inspector asked.

'No, I didn't, replied Eva-Lotta.

The chief inspector sighed, but then he reminded himself that a policeman's job is not an easy one. This interview with the girl had given them plenty to go on, even so. You couldn't expect to be handed the murderer's name on a plate.

Before he continued questioning Eva-Lotta he telephoned the police station and gave the order for every single inch of the Prairie to be scoured. The actual crime scene had been thoroughly searched, naturally, but a piece of paper can blow far away. The IOU must and would be found.

Afterwards Eva-Lotta had to tell him how she had found Gren. She swallowed hard, time after time, and spoke very quietly now. Her father rested his head in his hands so he didn't have to see the anxious look in her eyes.

But it would soon be over. The chief inspector had only a couple of questions left.

Eva-Lotta insisted that the murderer absolutely couldn't be anyone from this town, otherwise she would have recognized him.

The chief inspector asked:

'Do you think you would recognize him if you saw him again?'

'Yes,' said Eva-Lotta. 'I could pick him out of a thousand people.'

'You've never seen him before?'

'No,' said Eva-Lotta.

She hesitated for a split second.

'Well... kind of.'

The chief inspector's eyes widened. This interview was full of surprises.

'What do you mean, "kind of"?' he asked.

'I've seen his trousers.'

'You're going to have to explain that one,' said the chief inspector.

Eva-Lotta felt uncomfortable.

'Am I?' she asked.

'You know you are. Where were his trousers hanging?'

'They weren't hanging,' said Eva-Lotta. 'They were showing underneath a roller blind. The murderer was in them.'

The chief inspector grabbed the last remaining Danish pastry. He felt in need of something to give him strength. He wondered whether Eva-Lotta was quite as matter-of-fact as he had thought. Wasn't she starting to fantasise now?

'Let me see,' he said. 'The murderer's trousers were showing beneath a roller blind. Whose roller blind?'

'Gren's of course.'

'And you? Where were you?'

'I was on his ladder, outside. Kalle and I were both on it. Last Monday evening, about ten o'clock.'

The chief inspector didn't have any children, and at this moment he was heartily grateful.

'What on earth were you doing on Gren's ladder on Monday evening?' he asked. Then, guided by his new-found knowledge, he added: 'Oh, I get it, you were after another one of those Great Stonytotems, weren't you?'

Eva-Lotta gave him a stony look.

'Do you think Great Stonytotems grow on trees, Chief Inspector? There will only ever, ever, *ever* be one Great Stonytotem for all eternity!'

Then Eva-Lotta told him about their night-time walk over Gren's roof. The poor baker shook his head in amazement when he heard that. And people said it was easier to bring up girls!

'How did you know they were the murderer's trousers you saw?' asked the chief inspector.

'I didn't,' said Eva-Lotta. 'If I had I would have gone in and arrested him.'

'Yes, but you said...' interrupted the chief inspector, confused.

'No, I worked that out afterwards,' said Eva-Lotta. 'Because they were a pair of dark-green trousers, the same as the ones I saw on the path.'

'It could be a coincidence,' said the chief inspector. 'We mustn't jump to any hasty conclusions.'

'I haven't jumped,' said Eva-Lotta. 'I heard them arguing inside about IOUs, you see. The man with the trousers said: "See you Wednesday, usual place. Bring all my IOUs with you!" And how many green trousers do you think Gren has time to meet on any one single boring Wednesday, at a guess?'

The chief inspector was convinced Eva-Lotta was right. The puzzle pieces fitted. It was clear now. The motive, the time of day, the way it was done. There was only one thing remaining: to apprehend the murderer.

The chief inspector stood up and patted Eva-Lotta's cheek.

'Thank you very much,' he said. 'You've been a very good girl. You have helped us more than you think. Now, go away and forget all about it!'

'Yes, I will. Thanks,' said Eva-Lotta.

The chief inspector turned to Constable Björk.

'All we've got to do now is get hold of that Kalle,' he said. 'So he can confirm what Eva-Lotta has told us. Where can we find him?'

'Here,' came a confident voice from the balcony above the veranda.

The chief inspector looked up in astonishment and saw two heads, one light, one dark, poking above the balcony railing.

Knights of the White Roses never leave a comrade at

times of trouble, police interrogation or other ordeals. Like the baker, Kalle and Anders had wanted to be present at the questioning. But to be on the safe side, they thought it wise not to ask for permission first.

10

All the newspapers in the country had the murder on their front pages, and a great deal was written about Eva-Lotta's evidence. Her name wasn't mentioned, but they talked about 'the clever thirteen-year-old' a lot, and how her close observations at the murder scene had provided the police with such excellent information.

The local paper wasn't quite so discreet when it came to names. Naturally, every single person in the small town knew that the clever thirteen-year-old was none other than Eva-Lotta Lisander, and the editor could see no reason why her name shouldn't be printed in his paper. It was ages since he'd had such a juicy story, and he made the most of it. He wrote a lengthy, sentimental article about 'our friendly little Eva-Lotta, who today is playing among the flowers in her parents' garden and appears to have completely forgotten her terrible experience last Wednesday out on the windswept Prairie.'

And he went on, ecstatically: 'Yes, and where else is

she able to forget, where else is she able to feel safe, if not here—here, at home with her mother and father, here in the familiar surroundings of her childhood home, where the aroma of freshly baked bread from her father's bakery is a reminder of the security of everyday life that will not be destroyed by savage intrusion from the world of crime.'

He was very satisfied with this introduction. He went on to emphasize how clever Eva-Lotta had been, and what a detailed description she had given of the murderer. He didn't actually write 'murderer', but 'the man who is presumed to have the answer to the riddle.' He mentioned that Eva-Lotta was positive she would recognize the man in question if she were to run into him again, and he took extra care to point out that perhaps little Eva-Lotta Lisander would be the means by which a ruthless villain would be forced to meet his rightful punishment.

In fact, he wrote everything he shouldn't have written.

It was a very troubled Constable Björk who shoved the newspaper under the chief inspector's nose down at the police station. The chief inspector read it, and bellowed:

'How thoroughly irresponsible to write this kind of thing! Nothing less than irresponsible!'

Mr Lisander the baker used a stronger word when he came tearing into the newspaper offices a moment later. The veins on the sides of his head were throbbing with rage, and he thumped his fist on the editor's desk.

'It's criminal writing this kind of thing, don't you understand?!' he said. 'Have you any idea how dangerous this can be for my daughter?'

No, in all honesty, that hadn't actually occurred to the editor. Dangerous? In what way?

'Don't act as if you are more stupid than you already are, because that's not really necessary, you know,' said the baker. He hit the nail on the head there. 'Don't you understand that a man who can murder *once* can very easily do it again, if he feels it's necessary? And how *very* considerate of you to give out Eva-Lotta's name and address. Couldn't you have written her telephone number as well, so he can ring and book an appointment?'

Even Eva-Lotta thought the article was criminal, at least selected parts of it.

She sat in the bakery loft with Anders and Kalle, reading.

'"Friendly little Eva-Lotta who is today playing among the flowers in her parents' garden"—what stonking great tosh! Are they really allowed to write such drivel in the papers these days?'

Kalle took the paper from her and read the article for himself. Afterwards he shook his head, looking worried. He was still enough of a master detective to realize what a mistake the article was. But he didn't say that to the others.

The editor was right, however, when he wrote that

Eva-Lotta had recovered from her dreadful experience. She did still feel old, admittedly—almost fifteen years old—but fortunately she had the ability of the young to forget any unpleasantness, practically from one day to the next. It was only at night, when she was lying in bed, that her thoughts kept straying to the thing she would rather forget. She slept restlessly for the first few nights, and called out in her sleep, so her mother had to come in and wake her.

But during the bright, sunny daytime Eva-Lotta was as untroubled and happy as before. Her intention to be more ladylike and not take part in any more Wars of the Roses lasted precisely two days. After that she couldn't stand it any longer. She thought if she threw herself into really wild games, the quicker the other stuff would fade from her mind.

The police had stopped guarding the Mansion, but even before that happened, the Great Stonytotem had been carried off. Sworn to secrecy, Constable Björk had been given the task of fetching it from behind the cordoned-off area. After the questioning on the veranda, when explaining about the existence of the Great Stonytotem had become unavoidable, Anders took Constable Björk aside and asked him if he would be very kind and free the Great Stonytotem from its captivity. Constable Björk was happy to oblige. To be honest, he was curious to see what a Great Stonytotem looked like.

That is how the Great Stonytotem happened to be taken from its hiding place under police escort and handed over to the leader of the Whites. Right now it was in the chest of drawers in the bakery loft where the Whites kept all their trophies. But that was only a temporary solution. It would soon be moved.

Thinking it over, Anders decided it wasn't a good idea to hide it beside the pump in the courtyard of the castle ruins.

'I'd like him to be somewhere more exciting,' he said.

'Poor Great Stonytotem,' said Eva-Lotta. 'I think he's had enough of exciting places.'

'I mean a different kind of exciting place,' said Anders. He pulled open the drawer and looked fondly at the Great Stonytotem, lying in a cigar box on a bed of cotton wool. 'Much have your eyes seen, oh Great Stonytotem,' he said, and he felt more convinced than ever of its magical powers.

'I know,' said Kalle. 'We can hide him in one the Reds' houses.'

'What on earth do you mean?' said Eva-Lotta. 'Are we going to hand him back to the Reds of our own free will?'

'No,' said Kalle. 'But they can have him for a while and not know about it. If they don't know they've got him then it's exactly the same as if they haven't got him. And think how angry they'll be afterwards, when we tell them!'

Anders and Eva-Lotta realized what a brilliant idea this was. After a lively discussion about the various possibilities, they decided to hide the Great Stonytotem in Sixten's bedroom, and they made up their minds to go there instantly and search for a suitable place. They slid down the rope and sprang eagerly down to the narrow river and over the planks Eva-Lotta had put across the water especially for vital Roses' business. It was the quickest route to the Reds' headquarters in Sixten's garage.

Puffing and panting they arrived at the postmaster's house. Sixten, Benka and Jonte were sitting in the garden drinking blackcurrant squash and eating biscuits when the Whites came storming in. Anders passed on the joyful news that Eva-Lotta no longer refused to carry weapons, and as a result the Wars of the Roses could pick up where it left off. The Reds listened to this with the deepest satisfaction. Eva-Lotta's decision to become more ladylike had plunged them into gloom, and never before had they experienced anything so boring as the past few days.

Hospitably, Sixten invited his enemies to sit down and help themselves. The enemies didn't have to ask twice before Anders said, wily as a fox:

'Can't we drink it up in your room, Sixten?'

'What's the matter, have you got sunstroke?' his host asked politely. 'Sit indoors when it's such lovely weather?'

They drank squash and ate biscuits out of doors, in the lovely weather.

'I'd like to have a look at your small-bore rifle,' said Kalle afterwards.

The small-bore rifle which hung on the wall in Sixten's bedroom was his prize possession, and he had shown it to them over and over again until it was painful to see it. Kalle couldn't be more sick of seeing Sixten's small-bore rifle, but it was all in a good cause.

Sixten's face lit up.

'You want to look at my small-bore rifle?' he said. 'All right, you can.'

And he hurried off to the garage and fetched it.

'What?' said Kalle, disappointedly. 'Do you keep it in the garage these days?'

'Yes I do. Lucky it was so close to hand,' said Sixten, and he began to demonstrate his treasure to Kalle.

Anders and Eva-Lotta laughed so much they got biscuit crumbs caught in their throats. Eva-Lotta saw that a little female deception was required if they were ever going to get into Sixten's room that day.

She looked up at Sixten's bedroom window and said innocently:

'I bet you've got a good view from your room.'

'Yes, you can say that again,' said Sixten.

'If only those trees weren't so tall, I'm sure you'd be able to see all the way to the water tower,' said Eva-Lotta.

'But I can flipping well see the water tower now,' said Sixten.

'Yes, he flipping well can,' said Benka, loyal as ever.

'Can he?' said Eva-Lotta. 'No, you're joking.'

'Liar, liar, pants on fire,' said Anders and Kalle together. 'There's no way he can see the water tower.'

'Utter tosh,' said Sixten. 'Come with me and I'll show you the water tower, you squirts.'

He took the lead and all six filed into the house. A collie dog was asleep in the hall, out of the heat, and he leapt up barking as they trooped in.

'Down, Beppo. Down, boy,' said Sixten. 'It's only a couple of intellectually-challenged nincompoops who want to see the water tower.'

They carried on up the stairs to Sixten's room and he took them triumphantly over to the window.

'There,' he said, proudly. 'That's what I call a water tower. But you can call it what you like.'

'That showed you,' said Jonte.

'Yes, it did indeed,' said Eva-Lotta with a knowing smile. 'You can see the water tower. So what?'

'What do you mean?' asked Sixten, annoyed.

'I only mean—fancy being able to see a *whole* water tower,' Eva-Lotta laughed.

Anders and Kalle couldn't be less interested in the view. Their eyes were scouring the room, searching intently for a suitable hiding place for the Great Stonytotem.

'Nice room you've got here,' they said to Sixten, as if they hadn't been in it a hundred times before.

They circled the room, felt around Sixten's bed and casually pulled open his desk drawers.

Eva-Lotta valiantly endeavoured to keep the others by the window. She pointed at everything that could possibly be seen, and there certainly was plenty to be seen.

On the chest of drawers stood Sixten's globe.

Anders and Kalle had the idea at the same time. The globe—of course! They shot each other a look and nodded in confirmation.

They knew from a previous visit to Sixten's house that the globe could be unscrewed into two halves. Sixten occasionally amused himself by doing just that, and as a result the globe was rather worn around the Equator. Judging from Sixten's globe, large parts of Equatorial Africa were still undiscovered, they were so full of white patches.

There was a risk, naturally, that Sixten would happen to unscrew his globe and find the Great Stonytotem. Kalle and Anders were both aware of that. But what would the Wars of the Roses be if you didn't take risks?

'I think we've seen what we wanted to see,' said Anders pointedly to Eva-Lotta, and she left her place by the window.

'Yes, thanks, we've seen all the view we needed to see,' said Kalle, grinning contentedly. 'Come on, let's scram!'

'Wow-hoh-e-ror-e?' asked Eva-Lotta in curiosity.

'Tot-hoh-e gog-lol-o-bob-e,' answered Kalle.

'Gog-o-o-dod,' said Eva-Lotta.

Sixten glared at them when they started their totting nonsense, as he called it.

'Look in again when you feel you're desperate for more of the water tower,' was all he actually said.

'Yes, do that, why don't you?' said Jonte, his brown eyes looking sarcastic and superior.

'Vermin,' said Benka, by way of farewell.

The Whites trailed out through the door. It creaked in protest as they opened it.

'On your door you've got a hinge
All it seems to do is whinge,'

sang Anders. 'Why don't you put some oil on it?'

'Why don't you go home and stick your head in a bucket?' said Sixten.

The Whites returned to their headquarters. A hiding place had been found. Now all they had to do was decide when and how the Great Stonytotem would get there.

'When the full moon shines at midnight,' said Anders, in a spooky voice, 'The Great Stonytotem will be taken to its new resting place. And I'm the man to do it!'

Eva-Lotta and Kalle nodded approvingly. Naturally, the Whites would score an extra point if they managed to get into Sixten's room while he was lying there asleep.

'That sounds brilliant,' said Eva-Lotta, and she offered them a chocolate from a big box she was keeping in her chest of the drawers. She could eat herself sick with as many sweets as she liked because she had been given tons recently. As the editor had so correctly written in his article, along with all the other guff: 'Popular little Eva-Lotta is in the happy position of being able to accept tokens of affection from many sources. People, both familiar and unknown, are sending her presents as a sign that she is in their thoughts. Sweets, chocolates, toys and books are some of the items kind postmaster Pettersson has delivered from all her many friends, eager to show their sympathy since she so innocently became involved in this wretched tragedy.'

'And what will you do if Sixten wakes up?' asked Kalle.

That possibility didn't seem to bother Anders.

'I'll tell him I've gone there to sing him a lullaby and make sure he's nicely tucked in.'

'Oh, ha ha,' said Kalle. 'Listen, popular little Eva-Lotta, give me another chocolate and you'll be twice as popular.'

They scoffed the lot as they sat in their scruffy, cosy attic, making plans until the evening. They were jubilant about their new stunt against the Reds. This Wars of the Roses business was wonderful stuff! Eventually they left their headquarters. They had to get 'out in the field' as

Anders called it. You never knew, something useful could turn up. If nothing else, there was always the possibility of stirring up a minor scuffle with the Reds. As they slid down the rope Eva-Lotta said thoughtlessly:

'Ah yes, the happy games of childhood, childhood's hap...'

She stopped mid-sentence and turned as white as a sheet. Then she gave a sob and swiftly ran off.

She didn't play any more that day.

11

'Tonight's the night,' said Anders, a couple of days later.

For various reasons, the task of moving the Great Stonytotem to Sixten's globe had to be postponed. Firstly, it was because they wanted to wait for the full moon. It had to be a full moon, that was magical and ideal, and also it had the advantage of allowing them to find their way around a room without any kind of light. And secondly, it was because Sixten's two young aunts had come to stay in the postmaster's house.

'You'd have to be unhinged to go into a house with a little aunt in every corner, ready to pop out at you,' said Anders, when Kalle asked him if it was ever going to happen. 'You see, the more people there are in a house, the greater the risk that one of them wakes up and spoils everything.'

'Yes, aunts can be extraordinarily light sleepers,' Kalle admitted.

To his surprise, Sixten was bombarded with questions

about how his aunts were and how long they planned to stay. Finally, he got irritated.

'What's all this nagging about my aunts?' he said, when Anders brought them into the conversation for the tenth time. 'Are they in your way?'

'No, of course not,' said Anders, caught off guard.

'That's okay, then,' said Sixten. 'I think they're leaving on Monday. Pity, really, because I like them, especially Aunt Ada. And as long as they stay indoors with us and don't go rampaging about town, I can't see they're bothering anyone.'

After that answer Anders didn't think he could ask any more. It would have seemed suspicious.

But today was Monday, and Anders had seen the postmaster's wife take her two sisters to the morning train, and tonight it would be a full moon.

'Tonight's the night,' said Anders.

They were sitting among the lilac bushes in the baker's garden, eating freshly baked buns that Eva-Lotta had talked her father into giving them.

A minute earlier the Reds had walked past. They were on their way to their new headquarters in the Mansion, now the police had left. The Prairie was so tranquil it was as if its deep peace had never been disturbed. The Mansion was far too good a hideout for them to abandon it, and the Reds didn't want to waste any more time thinking about the awful thing that had happened near it.

'If you feel like taking a beating, come out to the Mansion,' shouted Sixten, as he walked past the baker's garden.

Eva-Lotta shuddered. She most definitely did not want to go out to the Mansion, not under any circumstances!

'Oh, I'm so full up,' groaned Kalle, after the Reds had disappeared and he had eaten his seventh bun.

'Nothing compared to me,' said Anders. 'But that's absolutely fine because we're having fish for dinner today.'

'Eating fish makes you intelligent,' Eva-Lotta reminded them. 'You should eat a little more, Anders.'

'Fat chance,' said Anders. 'First I want to know precisely how intelligent I will become and how much fish I have to eat.'

'That all depends on how intelligent you are before you start the experiment,' said Kalle. 'One little whale a week ought to be enough for you, Anders.'

When Anders had chased Kalle round the garden three times and peace was restored, Eva-Lotta said:

'I wonder if any more deliveries have come for me today. I don't understand what people are thinking. I've only had three kilos of chocolate over the last few days. I'll phone the post office and complain.'

'Don't mention chocolate,' said Anders, pulling a face. Kalle did the same. They had struggled bravely with the overwhelming amount of sweets and chocolate that had poured in for Eva-Lotta. Now they couldn't force down any more.

Eva-Lotta returned from the letterbox by the gate with a thick envelope in her hand. She tore it open and sure enough, there inside was a bar of chocolate—a huge, thick slab of it.

Anders and Kalle looked at it as if it had been cod liver oil.

'Oh crikey,' they said.

'There will come a day when you'll be glad of this,' Eva-Lotta said.

She broke the bar in two and made them take half each.

They took it to please her, but without the slightest hint of enthusiasm. They crammed the chocolate nonchalantly into their already-full trouser pockets.

'That's right,' said Eva-Lotta. 'Save it until there's a famine.'

She crumpled the envelope into a ball and threw it over the fence and into the road.

'Come on, let's cycle to the lake and go swimming,' said Kalle. 'There's hardly anything else we can get up to today.'

'You're right there,' said Anders. 'We might as well have a ceasefire until this evening. But then, just you wait.'

Two minutes later Benka came along, sent by Sixten,

to incite the Whites to battle using the foulest of insults, but by that time the garden was empty. There was only a little wagtail sitting on the see-saw, pecking up the crumbs.

At midnight, when the full moon was shining, Kalle and Eva-Lotta were fast asleep in their beds. But Anders was keeping watch. He had gone to bed as usual, like the others, and he was making the most artificial snores to fool his parents into thinking he was asleep. That had only resulted in his mother leaning over his bed and asking:

'What's wrong, boy, are you feeling ill?'

'Nope,' said Anders. After that he made sure he didn't snore quite so loudly.

Finally, when he could tell from his brothers' and sisters' gentle breathing and his parents' wheezing that everyone was asleep, he tiptoed quietly into the kitchen. His clothes were ready in a pile on a chair. He tugged off his nightshirt and stood there in the moonshine without a stitch on his thin, bony body. He listened anxiously in the direction of the bedroom, but all was still, and he quickly put on his clothes. Then he padded silently and calmly down the staircase. It didn't take him long to sprint to the bakery loft and collect the Great Stonytotem.

'Oh, Great Stonytotem,' he whispered, as he shut the drawer. 'Hold your powerful hand over this mission. I think I'm going to need it.'

The night air was chilly and he shivered in his thin clothes. The excitement also had something to do with it. It felt strange to be out here in the middle of the night while everyone else was asleep.

Holding the Great Stonytotem tight in his hand, he ran over the planks that were Eva-Lotta's bridge. The willows looked black beside the water, but the river glittered in the moonlight.

'Nearly reached our goal, oh Great Stonytotem,' he whispered, just in case the Great Stonytotem was getting impatient.

Yes, they would soon arrive at their destination. There was the postmaster's house, standing dark and silent as if it was sleeping. The grasshoppers were clicking, but otherwise there wasn't a sound.

Anders had counted on at least a couple of windows being open in the house, and he wasn't disappointed. It would be easy for Anders, who was good at gymnastics, to haul himself over the windowsill and into the kitchen. He shoved the Great Stonytotem in his pocket to have both hands free. It wasn't a particularly worthy place for the Great Stonytotem, but that couldn't be helped.

'Forgive me, oh Great Stonytotem,' said Anders.

His fingers prodded around in his pocket and he was taken by surprise when they closed around something squidgy that had once been a bar of chocolate. Anders wasn't feeling quite as full up as he had been earlier in the day, and he thought the squidgy lump would be very tasty right now. But he would save it as a reward for a job well done. First he had to do what he came for. He moved the Great Stonytotem to the other pocket and licked his fingers clean. Then he confidently heaved himself up on to the windowsill.

A low growling almost scared him out of his wits. Beppo! Not for one minute had he considered Beppo! And yet he should have realized the window was open for Beppo to go outside if he wanted.

'Beppo...' he whispered. 'Beppo, it's only me.'

When Beppo saw it was only one of those jokers his master used to bring into the house, his growling changed to a delighted woof.

'Oh, no, dear Beppo, please be quiet,' Anders implored.

But Beppo thought if you were glad you should show it by barking and wagging your tail, and he did both eagerly.

In desperation Anders took out the bar of chocolate and shoved it under Beppo's nose.

'You can have this, if only you'll shut up,' he whispered.

Beppo sniffed the chocolate, and because he concluded that the welcome ceremony had gone on as long as was expected, he stopped barking and lay down happily to enjoy the gooey treat the guest had given him, no doubt as a thank you for being clever enough to welcome him so loudly.

Anders breathed a sigh of relief and quietly, quietly opened the door into the hall. There was the staircase, now all he had to do...

Then someone appeared at the top. Someone was walking heavily down the stairs. It was the postmaster himself, in his long nightshirt. He had been woken up by Beppo's barking, and now he wanted to find out what had set him off.

Anders stood for a second as if paralysed, then in a flash he plucked up all his courage and dived in behind a couple of heavy overcoats that were hanging from the rack in a corner of the hall.

'If I don't have a nervous breakdown after this, you can call me Superman,' he said to himself.

Not until now had he thought that the postmaster and his family wouldn't take too kindly to someone barging through their window at night. Sixten wouldn't have blinked an eyelid, but then he was used to the Wars of the Roses, he was! The postmaster wasn't. Anders trembled at the thought of what the postmaster would do to him if he was discovered. He shut his eyes and said a silent prayer as the postmaster walked past the overcoats, muttering irritably to himself.

The postmaster opened the kitchen door. Beppo was lying down, looking at him in the moonlight.

'Well, boy,' said the postmaster. 'What are you barking for, in the middle of the night?'

Beppo didn't answer. He put his paw over the heap of delicious squidginess because his owner had such silly ideas. Only yesterday the postmaster had taken a lovely smelly bone away from Beppo, who had dropped it so nicely on the sitting-room carpet. Would he have the same approach to this squashy lump? Who could tell. To be on the safe side, Beppo yawned and tried to look as if nothing had happened. The postmaster calmed down, but he looked out of the window, just in case.

'Is there anyone there?' he called, nervously.

Only the night wind answered him. He couldn't hear Anders muttering behind the overcoats:

'No, no, there's no one here. Not even the tiniest flea, I can guarantee you that.'

Anders stood in his corner for a long time. He didn't move until he was certain the postmaster had gone back to sleep. He felt bored standing there, and soon it felt as if he had spent the best part of his youth behind those overcoats, whose itchy wool was tickling his nose. He was a person who like to be doing things, and waiting was something he hated. Finally, he couldn't bear it a minute longer. He stepped out of his prison and began slowly advancing up the stairs. He stopped on every step and listened, but there wasn't the slightest sound to be heard.

'This is going well,' said Anders, full of optimism as always.

It was Sixten's squeaking door that worried him. He lowered the handle and pushed gently. And guess what—the door didn't squeak at all! It opened smoothly and silently, and had obviously been oiled recently.

Anders laughed to himself. Sixten had oiled the door and caused his own downfall! Such kind enemies Anders had! All you had to do was point out a little inconvenience, and Bob's your uncle, they set about putting it right, so you could sneak in as easily as anything.

'Thanks, Sixten, very thoughtful of you,' thought Anders, and threw a look in the direction of Sixten's bed. There he was asleep, the poor thing, without an inkling that the Great Stonytotem would be taking up residence in his home this very night.

The globe was standing on the chest of drawers, lit up by the moonlight that was pouring in. Anders' nimble fingers soon unscrewed the two halves. Oh, what a truly magnificent place for a Great Stonytotem! Eagerly he took the trophy from his pocket and placed it in its new storage place.

'For a short time only, oh Great Stonytotem,' he said, when he had completed the job. 'For a short while you must be among the heathen tribe who obey not the law! But soon the White Roses will once again give you shelter among civilized Christian folk!'

A pair of scissors lay on the desk next to the globe, and when Anders saw them he had a brilliant idea. When you were in the presence of your sleeping enemy it was usual to cut off a corner of his cloak. That's what people did in the olden days, at least that's what it said in books. It was a fantastic way to show you had superiority over your enemy but were decent enough not to do him any harm. Then you could turn up the next day, wave the piece of cloak under your enemy's nose and say: 'Go down on your bare knees and thank me for your life, you cringing mongrel!'

And that is exactly what Anders intended to do. Sixten didn't have a cloak, naturally. But he had hair, a thick mop of red head hair. And Anders planned to cut off a piece of that hair. Oho, when the day came and the Great Stonytotem was safely tucked away somewhere else, the Reds would get the surprise of their lives! Because that's when they would learn the bitter truth about the Great Stonytotem and the globe. And they would also see the lock of hair that the leader of the White Roses had cut from the head of the leader of the Red Roses, as the full moon shone at midnight. A double triumph!

As it happened, the full moon wasn't shining on Sixten's bed. The bed was standing over in the corner, where it was pitch black. With the scissors in one hand, Anders felt his way across the room.

The unsuspecting leader of the Reds—there he was, with his hair spread out on the pillow. Anders took a gentle hold of a piece of Sixten's fringe, and cut it off.

A deafening scream ripped through the silence of the night. And it wasn't the scream of a young lad, but the shrill, piercing scream of a woman. Anders felt his blood turn to ice. He was gripped by a panic he had never known before, and he threw himself headlong towards the door. He leapt over the stair rail and slid down the banister at top speed, then flung open the kitchen door and in two great bounds was over by the window. He shot out over the windowsill as if the hounds of hell were after him. He pelted to the bridge over the river, and there he was forced to stop and catch his breath. He still had the tuft of hair in his hand—he hadn't dared let go of it.

He stood in the moonlight, panting and looking in disgust at what he was holding. These blonde curls undoubtedly belonged to an aunt, whichever one it could be. Clearly only one of them had left on the morning train. How was he to know that! And wasn't that precisely what he had said? It would be dead dangerous going into a house with an aunt in every corner. What a disgrace! What awful embarrassment! Going out for a piece of the Red leader's scalp, and coming back with a handful of hair from a little blonde aunt! Anders despaired as he stood there. This was the worst thing that had ever happened to him in his life. He decided not to tell a living soul. It would remain a ghastly secret that he would take with him to his grave.

He wanted to get rid of the tuft of hair as quick as he

could. He held his hand over the bridge railing and let the hair fall. The black water received his gift in silence. It burbled calmly under the arches of the bridge, just as it had always done.

Over at the postmaster's house, however, chaos had broken out. The postmaster and his wife had run anxiously in to Aunt Ada, and even Sixten came running down from the attic, where he had been moved since the aunts arrived.

Why on earth had Aunt Ada screamed so madly in the middle of the night, the postmaster wanted to know. Because there had been an intruder, said Aunt Ada. The postmaster switched on all the lights in the house, and they searched everywhere, but no intruder could be found anywhere. The silver cutlery was where it should be, not a single item was missing. Oh, what about Beppo? He had gone out into the garden as usual, they supposed, and if there really had been an intruder Beppo would have barked and made no end of noise, didn't Aunt Ada realize that? She had been dreaming, that was all! They patted her comfortingly and said she must go back to bed and get some sleep.

But when Aunt Ada was alone, she was too afraid to sleep. No one could tell her there hadn't been an intruder in her room! She lit a cigarette to calm her nerves. Then she took out her mirror to see if the terror of the night visit had left its mark on her lovely face.

Then she saw it. The visit *had* left its mark. She had been given a new hairstyle. A large chunk of hair had been cut off. Quite unexpectedly she had been given a perky little fringe.

She stared at the mirror in horror, but eventually a wide smile spread over her face. Someone, whoever it might be, had been foolish enough to break into the house in the middle of the night, simply to get a lock of her hair!

Men had committed foolish deeds before for Aunt Ada's sake, so she was used to it, but this was the daftest of the lot. She wondered for a while who her unknown admirer could be, but it was, and remained, a mystery to her. Whoever he was, Aunt Ada decided to forgive him. She wouldn't betray him, either. They could go on believing she had dreamed it all.

Aunt Ada sighed and climbed into bed. Tomorrow she would go to the hairdresser's and get the mutilated fringe trimmed properly.

12

A new day dawned and in the baker's garden, Kalle and Eva-Lotta had been waiting eagerly since early morning for Anders to appear and give them a report about the night's events. But the hours passed and no Anders came.

'Odd,' said Kalle. 'He can't have been taken prisoner again, can he?'

They were just about to go and search for him when he finally turned up. He wasn't running like he usually did, and his face was a strange shade of green.

'You look miserable,' said Eva-Lotta. 'Are you one of those "victims of the heat", as it says in the paper?'

'I'm a victim of boiled fish,' said Anders. 'I'm allergic to fish. I've told Mum I don't know how many times, and here's the living proof.'

'What do you mean?' asked Kalle.

'I've been throwing up all night. In and out of bed like a yo-yo.'

'What about the Great Stonytotem?' Kalle said. 'Does that mean it's still in the chest of drawers?'

'Never fear, my friend! I got that done before it started,' said Anders. 'I do my duty, whatever abominable pestilence rages inside me. The Great Stonytotem is in Sixten's globe!'

Kalle and Eva-Lotta's eyes shone.

'Not bad going,' said Kalle. 'Tell us! Did Sixten wake up?'

'All right, all right. Calm down and I'll tell you,' said Anders.

The three of them went and sat on Lotta's home-made bridge. It was cool down there and the trees gave a pleasant shade. They dangled their legs in the warm water. Anders said it had a calming effect on the fish in his stomach.

'Maybe it wasn't only the fish, when I come to think about it,' he said. 'Maybe it was nerves as well, because last night I entered the house of horrors.'

'Tell us everything, from the beginning,' said Eva-Lotta.

So Anders did. Very dramatically he described his encounter with Beppo and how he had kept him quiet. Kalle and Eva-Lotta shuddered and cheered in turns. They were an ideal audience and Anders enjoyed telling them the story.

'So you see, if I hadn't given Beppo the chocolate, I'd have been snookered,' he said.

Then he described the even more terrifying encounter with the postmaster.

'Couldn't you have chucked him some chocolate as well?' said Kalle.

'No, Beppo ate it all,' Anders said.

'Then what happened?' asked Eva-Lotta.

Anders told them everything: about how Sixten's door hadn't squeaked but how Sixten's aunt had, so loudly that his blood had turned to ice, and how he'd had to run out into the night in a tearing hurry. The only thing he didn't mention was the aunt's chopped-off piece of fringe he had deposited in the river.

Kalle and Eva-Lotta thought it was more exciting than any adventure story they had ever heard, and they were only too glad to hear all the details over and over again.

'What a night,' said Eva-Lotta, when Anders had finally finished.

'Yes, and it's not so surprising if I'm a wreck at such a young age,' said Anders. 'But the main thing is, the Great Stonytotem is where it should be.'

Kalle kicked his feet about wildly in the water.

'Yes! The Great Stonytotem is in Sixten's globe,' he said. 'Can you imagine *anything* more fantastic than that!'

No, Anders and Eva-Lotta certainly couldn't. And their joy increased when they spotted Sixten, Benka and Jonte prowling along the riverbank.

'Ah, look at those pretty white roses all lined up,' said Sixten, as he reached the planks.

Benka thought he might as well try tipping the White Roses into the water, but Sixten stopped him. The Reds hadn't come to fight, they had come to complain instead.

According to the rules of the Wars of the Roses, the side that had the Great Stonytotem in their possession were obliged to give the other side a vague idea of where the trophy could be found. A tiny, tiny hint, at the very least! But had the White's done that? No! It was true that their leader, when he was being tickled, had blurted out something about the narrow path behind the Mansion, and just to be sure the Reds had spent all of yesterday scouring the entire area for a second time. But now they were convinced the Whites had put the Great Stonytotem in a different hiding place, and they insisted the Whites give them a reasonable clue. They were friendly, but determined.

Anders stepped down into the water. It didn't even reach his knees now. He stood there, legs apart, his hands on his hips and his dark eyes glittering in amusement.

'Yes, you can have your clue,' he said. 'Seek in the very centre of the earth!'

'Thanks, that was so kind of you,' said Sixten sarcastically. 'Shall we start here or up at the Polar Circle?'

'What a very helpful clue,' said Jonte. 'Our grand-children will find the Great Stonytotem before they go to their graves, I'm sure.'

'Yes, and think of the blisters they'll get from all that digging,' said Benka.

'Use your brains, Reds. If you've got any, that is,' said Anders. He added dramatically: 'If the leader of the Reds goes home and searches the centre of the earth, all will be revealed!'

Kalle and Eva-Lotta splashed their legs exaggeratedly in the water and laughed ecstatically.

'Exactly! Search the very centre of the earth,' they said, looking mysterious.

'Foul vermin,' said Sixten.

The Reds went home and began an extensive digging operation in the postmaster's garden. They dug all afternoon and prodded and poked about in places that might have the slightest possibility of hiding the Great Stonytotem. Eventually the postmaster came out and asked if it was really necessary for his lawn in particular to be utterly destroyed, or could they possibly do him the courtesy of wrecking somebody else's garden.

'And by the way, Sixten, I think you ought to find out what Beppo's up to,' he said finally.

'Hasn't Beppo come back yet?' asked Sixten, looking worried. He dropped the spade. 'Where on earth can he be?'

'That's exactly what I thought you could find out,' said his father.

Benka and Jonte had to go with him, of course, and

they weren't the only ones who wanted look for Beppo. Anders, Kalle and Eva-Lotta, who for the past hour had been hiding behind the hedge, watching the Reds slogging away, stepped out and offered their assistance. Sixten accepted gratefully. There were no enemies in the hour of need.

United as one, the whole party set off.

'He never usually goes missing,' said Sixten, looking rattled. 'Not for more than an hour or two, at least. But now he's been gone since eleven last night.'

'No, more like twelve,' said Anders. 'Because —'

He stopped abruptly and blushed violently.

'OK, since about twelve,' said Sixten absent-mindedly. Then he suddenly looked at Anders suspiciously.

'Hang on, how do you know that?'

'I'm one of those people who can sense these things,' said Anders, hastily. He hoped Sixten wouldn't cross-examine him further, because naturally he couldn't explain that he had seen Beppo in the kitchen at around midnight, when he was coming in with the Great Stonytotem, and that the dog had disappeared when he fled out of the window about an hour later.

'Well, how lucky we've found a fortune teller, just when we need one,' said Sixten. 'Would you be kind enough as to fortune tell where Beppo is right now?'

But Anders replied that he could only tell fortunes when it concerned the future, not the place.

'What time will we find Beppo, then?' Sixten was keen to know.

'We'll find him in roughly an hour,' said Anders, confidently. But there his fortune telling let him down. It didn't turn out to be quite that easy.

They looked everywhere. They searched the whole town. They asked people who owned dogs that Beppo used to go and say hello to. They asked everyone they met. But no one had seen Beppo. He had disappeared.

Sixten didn't say much. He walked around, sniffing, but on no account must the others see. He just blew his nose more often.

'Something must have happened to him,' he kept saying. 'He's never gone missing like this before.'

The others tried to comfort him.

'No, nothing's happened to him,' they said. But they weren't nearly as convinced as they sounded.

They walked in silence for a long time.

'He was such a nice dog,' Sixten said at last, his voice cracking. 'He understood everything you told him.'

Then he had to blow his nose again.

'Stop saying that,' said Eva-Lotta. 'You make it sound as if you think he's dead.'

Sixten didn't answer, but he sniffed loudly.

'He had very faithful eyes,' said Kalle. 'I mean, he *has* very faithful eyes,' he added hastily.

Then it was quiet again for a long time. When it got a

bit too much, Jonte said:

'Yes, dogs are lovely animals.'

They were on their way home by this time. There was no point in looking any longer. Sixten walked ahead of the others, kicking a stone in front of him. They understood how sad he was.

'What if Beppo has come home, Sixten, while we've been out looking for him?' said Eva-Lotta positively.

Sixten stopped in the middle of the street.

'If he has,' he said. 'If Beppo has come home, then I'll be a better person from now on. Oh, what a good person I will be! I'll wash behind my ears every day and...'

He began running with renewed hope. The others followed him, wishing desperately they would see Beppo waiting by the gate and barking as they ran up to the postmaster's house.

But there was no Beppo waiting. Sixten's generous promise to wash behind his ears every day hadn't had any effect on the powers that controlled a dog's life and movements. The hope had already drained from his voice as he called to his mum, who was sitting on the veranda:

'Has Beppo come back yet?'

She shook her head.

Sixten went quiet and sat down on the lawn. The others followed, a little uncertainly. They gathered round him without a word, because they could find no words to say, however hard they tried.

'I've had him ever since he was a tiny little puppy,' Sixten explained softly. They had to understand that if you've had a dog since he was a tiny little puppy then you had the right to snivel when that dog went missing.

'Do you know what he did once?' Sixten went on, as if to torture himself. 'It was when I came home from hospital, after I'd had my appendix out. Beppo met me at the gate, and he was so pleased to see me that he knocked me over and my stitches came open.'

Everyone was touched by this. A dog really couldn't show more proof of his affection than to knock his owner over and make the stitches burst open after his appendix operation.

'Yes, dogs are lovely animals,' Jonte said again.

'Especially Beppo,' said Sixten, blowing his nose.

Looking back, Kalle never knew what made him go and look in the postmaster's woodshed. It was stupid, really, he thought, because if Beppo had been locked in there by mistake then he would have barked until someone came to let him out.

But even if there was no sensible reason for Kalle to go and look in the woodshed, he did it anyway. He opened the door wide and the light streamed in. And there in a corner lay Beppo. He wasn't moving and for a stomach-churning moment Kalle was sure he was dead. But as he approached, Beppe lifted his head with an effort and whined slowly. Then Kalle shot out and yelled at the top of his voice:

'Sixten! Sixten! He's here, he's in the woodshed!'

'My Beppo! My poor little Beppo,' said Sixten, his voice shaking. He kneeled beside his dog and Beppo looked up at him, as if he wanted to ask his master why he hadn't come for him sooner. He had been lying here for an eternity and had been too ill to bark. Oh, how ill he had been! He tried to tell his master, and it sounded so indescribably pitiful.

'Listen, he's crying,' said Eva-Lotta, and she started crying as well.

Yes, Beppo was ill, and no mistake. He lay in sea of his own vomit and muck, and was too weak to move. All he did was lick Sixten's hand. He wanted to thank him because now he didn't have to suffer alone.

'I've got to get the vet, fast,' said Sixten.

But when he stood up Beppo whined fretfully.

'He's afraid you're going to leave him,' said Kalle. 'I'll run and get the vet instead.'

'Tell him to get a move on,' said Sixten. 'And tell him it's about a dog with rat poisoning.'

'How do you know?' asked Benka.

'Oh, I know all right,' said Sixten. 'I can see for myself. It's that flipping butcher's, they put out a plant called sea squill, to kill the rats. Beppo goes there sometimes and they give him a bone.'

'Can Beppo... can dogs die from that?' asked Anders, his eyes wide open in fear.

'Shut up!' said Sixten angrily. 'Not Beppo! Beppo's not going to die. I've had him ever since he was a tiny little puppy. Oh Beppo, why did you have to go and find rat poison?'

Beppo licked his hand weakly and didn't answer.

13

Kalle slept restlessly that night. He dreamed he was out looking for Beppo again. He was alone and wandering along dark deserted roads that stretched endlessly before him and vanished into a frightening gloom way off in the distance. He was waiting for someone to come along, someone he could ask about Beppo, but there was no one. The whole world was empty, dark and desolate. Suddenly it wasn't Beppo he was looking for, it was something else, something much more important, but he couldn't remember what. He felt he *had* to remember it, as if his life depended on it, but he couldn't think of it. He was in such a turmoil that he woke up.

Thank heavens it was only a dream! He looked at the clock. Five a.m. In that case he'd better try and go back to sleep. He burrowed his head into the pillow and tried, but it was strange, he couldn't get the dream out of his head. Even when he was awake it felt as if there was something he simply had to remember. It was tucked away in his brain, waiting to come to the surface. A miniscule patch of cells right at the back of his brain knew what it was. He scratched his head and muttered angrily:

'Okay, out with it then!'

But nothing came to him and Kalle got fed up trying. Eventually that lovely drowsy feeling came creeping over him.

Then, just as he was half asleep, that miniscule patch of cells decided to reveal what they had been working on. It was one sentence, that was all. And Anders was saying it.

'If I hadn't given Beppo the chocolate, I'd have been snookered.'

Kalle shot upright in bed. Instantly he was wide awake.

"If I hadn't given Beppo the chocolate, I'd have been snookered," he repeated over and over to himself.

What was so special about that? Why was it so crucial to remember that sentence in particular?

Because... because... there was the awful possibility that...

When he had got that far he lay down and pulled the quilt over his head with a groan.

'Kalle Blomkvist,' he warned himself. 'Don't start that detective business again, please! We agreed we were finished with all that bunkum!'

Now he would go to sleep. He really would!

'I'm a victim of boiled fish.'

Once again it was Anders' voice he heard. Holy moly,

was it too much to ask to be left in peace! Why was Anders here, jabbering away at him? Couldn't he stay in his own home and entertain himself, if he was so desperately in need of a chat?

Now nothing helped. Those dreadful thoughts demanded to be heard. He couldn't hold them back any longer.

What if it wasn't the fish that had made Anders throw up? Boiled fish can be disgusting, Kalle agreed, but it didn't usually make you vomit all night. And what if it wasn't sea squill Beppo had eaten? What if it was... what if it could possibly be... poisoned chocolate!

Kalle made another attempt to stop himself.

I see the master detective has been reading the newspapers again, he sneered at himself. Been keeping up to date with the latest crime stories, has he? So what if it has happened before, what if someone *has* been killed by eating poisoned chocolate, that doesn't mean to say that every single blooming bar of chocolate is stuffed full of arsenic!

He lay still for a while, thinking. And the thoughts were alarming.

There might be others, apart from me, who have read the papers and followed the crime stories, he thought. Someone else could very easily have done that. Someone wearing green trousers, and who is afraid. That some-one might also have read the article about Eva-Lotta, where it mentioned all the chocolate and sweets she was getting through the post. The article that said Eva-Lotta might be the means of catching the murderer. Holy macaroni, think if that was true!

Kalle leapt out of bed. The other half of the bar of chocolate—he had it! He had totally forgotten. Now, where was it?

It was there in his trouser pocket, of course. The blue trousers he was wearing the other day. He hadn't worn them since. That was lucky, incredibly lucky—if it was as he suspected.

You can imagine all sorts of things when you're lying awake in the early hours of the morning. It makes the most improbable thing seem probable. When Kalle was on his feet, still in his pyjamas and standing inside the small room that doubled as his wardrobe and his laboratory, and the early morning sun was streaming in through the window, he thought again what an idiot he was. It was just his imagination, all this. Of course it was—same as usual!

'But, even so...' he said. 'A little routine investigation won't hurt.'

His imaginary listener, who had been keeping out of the way for so long, was clearly only waiting for these words. He came galloping up, eager to see what the master detective was doing.

'And what is the master detective planning now?' he asked, awestruck.

'As I said—a little routine investigation.'

Suddenly Kalle was a master detective again. It couldn't be helped. He hadn't been able to be one for *ages*. But on the other hand, he hadn't really wanted to. When real life intervened he hadn't wanted to be a detective any more. But at this very minute he was so utterly convinced there were grounds for his suspicions that he fell helplessly into the old role.

He took the half bar of chocolate out of his trouser pocket and showed it to his invisible listener.

'For a number of reasons I suspect this bar of chocolate contains arsenic.'

His imaginary listener shrank back in horror.

'As you are aware, this kind of thing has happened before,' went on the master detective. 'There is something called copycat crime. It's very common. A criminal gets an idea for a crime when he hears about one that has already been committed.'

'But how can you be sure there really is arsenic in it?' asked the imaginary listener, looking uncertainly at the chocolate.

'Simple. You do a little test,' explained the master detective. 'The Marsh arsenic test. And that is what I intend to do now.'

His imaginary listener looked around the small room in admiration.

'An excellent laboratory you have here, Mr Blomkvist,'

he said. 'Mr Blomkvist is a skilful chemist, I see.'

'Well, I don't know about skilful, but I have spent a large part of my long life studying chemistry,' said the master detective. 'Chemistry and forensics go hand in hand, you understand, my young friend!'

His poor parents, had they been present, could most definitely have confirmed that much of Kalle's long life had indeed been spent on chemistry experiments in this walk-in wardrobe he called his laboratory. Except they might have expressed it differently. They probably felt it would be closer to the truth to say he had repeatedly tried to blow himself, and the house to smithereens, to satisfy an eagerness for research that was way beyond his ability.

But the imaginary listener was not nearly as sceptical as Kalle's parents. He watched in interest as the master detective took a whole array of equipment down from a shelf. They included a Bunsen burner and various glass pipes and jars.

'That test you were talking about, Mr Blomkvist, how is it done?' he asked, keen to learn.

The master detective was only too happy to teach him.

'What we need first of all is a hydrogen apparatus,' he said, trying to sound like a professor. 'I happen to have one. It is, quite simply, a jar, and in that jar I place some zinc in sulphuric acid. That creates hydrogen gas, you know. If we introduce arsenic in any form, a gas called arsine gas, or AsH_3, is produced. The gas goes through this tube and into a pipe where it is dried with anhydrous calcium chloride. Then it passes through this narrower tube which we heat with a spirit lamp. And then, you see, the arsenic sticks to the inside of the glass tube like a silvery-black coating. The so-called arsenic mirror, which I presume you have heard about, my young friend?'

His young friend had heard about nothing of the kind, but he followed the detective's preparations in suspense.

'But remember,' said the master detective, as he finally lit the spirit lamp. 'I haven't said the chocolate contains arsenic. This is simply a routine experiment I'm doing, and I sincerely hope my suspicions are unfounded.'

The sunny room fell quiet. The master detective was so involved with what he was doing that he quite forgot his young friend. By now the glass pipe had warmed up. Kalle crumbled a piece of the chocolate and dropped the pieces through a funnel into the hydrogen apparatus.

Then he held his breath, and waited.

Crikey, there it was! The arsenic mirror! The sickening proof that he was right. He stared at the glass tube as if he couldn't believe his eyes. Deep inside he had been doubtful, but now there could be no doubt. This meant... something truly horrendous.

He was shaking as he switched off the spirit lamp. His imaginary listener had gone—vanished the very moment

Kalle changed from a skilful master detective into a frightened Kalle.

Anders was woken a moment later by somebody whistling the White Roses' signal under his window. He poked a sleepy face through the pot plants to see who it was. There stood Kalle, outside the shoemaker's workshop, waving at him.

'Where's the fire?' asked Anders. 'What do you mean by waking people up at this hour?'

'Stop wittering and come down,' said Kalle. And when Anders finally came down, Kalle stared at him seriously, and asked: 'Did you try that chocolate before you gave it to Beppo?'

Anders looked at him in amazement.

'Did you come here at seven in the morning to ask me that?' he said.

'Yes, because there was arsenic in it,' said Kalle, calmly.

Anders' face grew pale and his jaw dropped.

'I don't remember,' he whispered. 'Yes I do, I licked my fingers . . . I'd pushed the Great Stonytotem right into that gunk I had in my pocket. Are you totally sure . . .'

'Yes,' said Kalle, abruptly. 'And now we're going to the police.'

Quickly he told Anders about the experiment and the awful truth it had revealed. They thought about Eva-Lotta, and felt more horrified than they had ever done before in their young lives. Eva-Lotta must not know about this. She must be kept in the dark until later, they were agreed on that.

Anders also thought of Beppo.

'I'm the one who has poisoned him,' he said. 'If Beppo dies, I can never look Sixten in the face again.'

'Beppo won't die. You heard what the vet said,' Kalle said, to comfort him. 'He's been given loads of medicine, had his stomach pumped, and all sorts of things. And surely it was better that Beppo ate the chocolate, rather than you or Eva-Lotta?'

'Or you,' said Anders.

They both shuddered.

'One thing's for sure,' said Anders, as they made their way to the police station.

'What?' said Kalle.

'You've got to take this case on, Kalle, otherwise it'll be chaos. I've been saying that all along.'

14

'This murder *must* be solved,' said the chief inspector, slapping his hand on the table.

For fourteen days he had been working on this particularly complicated case, and now he had to leave. The national police force had a huge area to cover, and there was work waiting for him elsewhere. Still, he left three of his men behind, and it was these men he had called to an early morning meeting at the police station, along with the local police.

'As far as I can make out,' he went on. 'The only concrete result after fourteen days of investigation is that nobody dares to go out wearing dark-green trousers.'

He shook his head despondently. They had all worked very hard indeed and followed up every imaginable lead, but the solution seemed as far away as when they had first begun. The murderer had appeared out of thin air and vanished back into thin air again. No one had seen him apart from one person: Eva-Lotta.

The public had done their best to help. A great deal of information had come in about people who usually walked about in dark-green trousers—and some even mentioned blue, green and brown trousers, just in case. And only yesterday the chief inspector had received an anonymous letter telling him that 'Tailor Andersson's lad be a right little tearaway and he's got black trousers. Lock the blighter up.'

'When they start asking you to arrest people because they're wearing black trousers, then it's not surprising that every pair of dark-green ones disappears like magic,' said the chief inspector, and he laughed.

Eva-Lotta had been summoned to the police station a couple of times to see if she could identify a few individuals the chief inspector wanted to take a closer look at. The suspects concerned had been lined up alongside dozens of others, all dressed more or less the same, and afterwards Eva-Lotta had been asked if any of them was the man she had bumped into on the Prairie.

'No, none of them,' Eva-Lotta had said every time.

She had also looked through masses of photographs the police had shown her, but there was no one there she recognized, either.

'And they look like such nice men,' she said, looking closely at pictures of killers and thieves.

Every single person who lived on Riffraff Hill had been asked if they had noticed anything in particular about Gren and the company he kept. The police were particularly keen to know if they had seen anything unusual on the Monday night before the murder, when the man in the dark-green trousers had supposedly visited Gren. And sure enough, everyone had noticed something colossally unusual on the evening in question. It had been absolute bedlam on Riffraff Hill that night, as if at least ten murderers were about to do each other some damage. That sounded most interesting. But pretty soon it became clear to the chief inspector that it was only the Roses who had caused the commotion. Several people, among them Kalle Blomkvist, had reported hearing a car start up and drive away at the time in question. And it turned out not to be Doctor Forsberg's car, which he had used when visiting Fredrik the Foot's house that evening.

Constable Björk had teased Kalle for not investigating that car better.

'And you the master detective,' he said. 'You should have sprinted up there and made a note of the number plate. How much effort are you actually putting into your job, these days?'

'I had three stark staring-mad Reds after me,' said Kalle in his defence, but rather shamefully at the same time.

The police had worked day and night trying to contact Gren's clients. They had managed to trace most of the names on the IOUs they had taken from Gren's house, and it became apparent that the people involved came from over the country.

'A man with a car—it's likely,' said the chief inspector, and he shook himself like angry terrier. 'He can just as easily live a thousand kilometres from here. He could have had the car parked near the Mansion and run back there immediately afterwards, driven off and been well on his way before we even knew what had happened.'

'Yes, he certainly couldn't have chosen a better meeting place than out by the Mansion,' said Constable Björk. 'The roads around there are completely deserted, and there's not a soul living out there, so no one could have seen him or heard his car.'

'Which clearly indicates the culprit knew the area, don't you think?' said the chief inspector.

'Perhaps,' said Constable Björk. 'But it can also be pure chance that it happened to be just there.'

There had been a thorough search for tyre marks on all the roads around the Mansion immediately after the murder. But there were none. The downpour had been a great help to the culprit.

And how they had looked for that dropped IOU! Every bush, every stone, every clump of grass had been searched. But the fateful paper had gone missing, and stayed missing.

'Vanished without trace, just like the murderer,'

sighed the chief inspector. 'If only the fellow would give us *some* sign of life!'

At that moment a couple of very noisy boys' voices were heard coming from the station reception. From the sound of it, they were demanding to see the chief inspector, because they could hear they young special constable out there explaining that the chief inspector was in a meeting and must not be disturbed.

The boys' voices became more insistent.

'We've *got* to see him, I'm telling you!'

Constable Björk recognized Anders' voice, and he stood up and walked out of the room.

'Oh, Constable Björk!' said Anders, as soon as he saw him. 'It's about this murder. Kalle has taken over now and...'

'No I haven't!' protested Kalle, indignantly. 'But...'

Constable Björk looked at them disapprovingly.

'I thought I told you this is nothing for young lads and master detectives.' He said. 'You can feel completely confident that the police are taking care of it. Now, go home!'

That made Anders angry, even with Constable Björk, who he admired tremendously.

'Go home?' he shouted. 'Go home, and let the murderer poison the whole town with arsenic?'

Kalle came to his assistance. He brought out a carefully-wrapped bar of chocolate and said in a sombre voice:

'Constable Björk, someone sent poisoned chocolate to Eva-Lotta.'

He looked pleadingly at the tall police officer who was standing there, trying to block his way. And suddenly Constable Björk was no longer blocking his way.

'Come in,' he said, and pushed the boys ahead of him.

There was silence when Kalle and Anders had finished telling their story. A long, long silence. Then the chief inspector said:

'Was it me who said something about wanting a sign of life from the murderer?'

He weighed the chocolate in his hand. This wasn't exactly the sign of life he had been expecting.

Then he looked questioningly at Anders and Kalle. There was just a chance these two youngsters had got hold of the wrong end of the stick. He didn't know how reliable Kalle's chemistry experiment was, or whether he could believe in his theory about the arsenic mirror. He might have let his imagination run away with him. Never mind, a technical analysis would provide an answer. That business with the dog was undeniably odd. It would have been helpful to have a sample from the other half of the bar of chocolate, the one the dog had eaten, but both boys assured him that yesterday evening they had helped clear away the mess the dog had made, and they couldn't have done more to wipe out every trace. As if that wasn't bad enough, Eva-Lotta had thrown away the envelope the chocolate came in, so the boys said. That kid had a liking for chucking important documents around, thought the chief inspector. But how was she to know the envelope would turn out to be so significant? Oh well, they would look for it, of course, but they were unlikely to find it.

He turned to Anders.

'I don't suppose you saved even the tiniest sliver of your half, did you?' he asked.

Anders shook his head.

'No, Beppo had all of it. I only licked what was left on my fingers.'

'Okay. What about your trouser pocket, then? Can there be any chocolate left in there?'

'Mum washed the trousers yesterday,' said Anders.

'Pity,' said the chief inspector.

He was quiet for a while, then he fixed his eyes on Anders.

'There's one thing I'm sitting here thinking about,' he said. 'There was something you had to do in the postmaster's kitchen last night, you said. You climbed into the kitchen when everyone was asleep. To an old policeman that sounds rather worrying. Could you possibly tell me what you were doing there?'

'Um, you see...' Anders squirmed in his seat.

'Well?' said the chief constable.

'It was the Great Stonytotem, you see…'

'Oh no, don't tell me he's mixed up in all this again,' groaned the chief inspector. 'That Great Stonytotem is starting to look very suspicious, if you ask me. He makes an appearance every time something happens.'

'I was going to put him in Sixten's globe,' said Anders, by way of explanation.

Kalle interrupted him with a yell.

'The Great Stonytotem!' he shouted. 'There might be chocolate on him! Anders shoved him into the squidgy chocolate he had in his pocket!'

A wide smile spread across the chief inspector's face.

'I think it is about time Mr Great Stonytotem paid us a visit,' he said.

And that was how the Great Stonytotem found himself under police escort yet again. Constable Björk hurried off to the postmaster's house, with Kalle and Anders close behind.

'The Great Stonytotem is getting very spoilt,' said Kalle. 'He'll soon be demanding a mounted police escort every time he's moved from one place to another.'

Despite the macabre reason for collecting the Great Stonytotem, and despite the memories it must stir up in their young minds, they couldn't help seeing it just a little from a White Roses' perspective. Thanks to the discovery that it was Anders who had poisoned Beppo— quite unknowingly, of course—the Great Stonytotem's secret hiding place in Sixten's globe would be revealed to the Reds. They would have to tell Sixten everything, and that meant he would immediately want to take possession of the trophy. But now the police had intervened and taken the Great Stonytotem under their protection. And however bad things were as far as Eva-Lotta and Beppo were concerned, Anders and Kalle couldn't help thinking that this was an excellent solution.

'When you think about it, the Great Stonytotem is a lifesaver,' said Kalle. 'Because if you hadn't gone and put him in the globe, Anders, Beppo would never have eaten the chocolate. And if Beppo hadn't eaten the chocolate, something a million times worse would have happened. You can't be sure everyone tolerates arsenic the way Beppo does.'

Both Constable Björk and Anders agreed.

'The Great Stonytotem deserves our admiration,' said Constable Björk, as he opened the postmaster's garden gate.

Beppo was lying in a basket on the veranda, still weak but undeniably alive. Sixten was sitting beside him, looking at him with eyes brimming with love and adoration. He'd had that dog ever since it had been a tiny little puppy, after all, and he planned on having him for many years to come.

When he heard the gate he looked up, and his eyes

widened in astonishment.

'Hello, Sixten,' said Constable Björk. 'I've come to collect the Great Stonytotem.'

15

How quickly is a murder forgotten? Very quickly, sad to say. People talk for a while—talk and try to guess who did it and complain that the police aren't doing enough. Then all of a sudden it isn't interesting any more. They start talking about something else, they get afraid and worked up about other things instead.

The ones who forget most quickly are the youngsters, the kind who have to fight the Wars of the Roses, the champions of the Great Stonytotem. They have so much to think about, so much to do. Who was it who said the summer holidays are long? Wrong, wrong, wrong! The summer holidays are so pitifully, disappointingly short that it makes you want to weep. You must make the most of every single second. You can't allow the thought of a murky act of violence to cast its shadow over the last sun-drenched week of the summer holidays!

Their mothers don't forget quite so quickly. They keep their little, fair-haired daughters at home for a time.

They don't dare to let them out of their sight. They peer anxiously through the window when they can't hear the usual racket their sons make outside. From time to time they go rushing out to convince themselves that nothing disastrous has happened to their little darlings. And for a long time they search everything that arrives in the post to make certain new dangers aren't lurking there. But in the end they get tired of worrying. They must try to focus their minds on something else. And their sons and daughters, who have found the extra attention a lot of bother, breathe a deep sigh of relief and return to their old battlefields and playgrounds, which have for a time been out of bounds.

The police don't forget, although it might look that way. They carry on beavering quietly away, despite all the disappointments, despite all the information that has to be dismissed as unhelpful, all the important documents that have gone missing, and despite the fact that at times it seems decidedly meaningless carrying on. The police keep on working—and they don't forget.

There is someone else who never forgets: the murderer. He remembers what he has done. He remembers it when he goes to bed at night and when he gets up in the morning, and all the long hours in between. He remembers it every moment of every day and night, and it follows him into his restless sleep.

And he is afraid. He is afraid when he goes to bed at

night and when he gets up in the morning, and all the long hours in between. He is afraid every moment of every day and night, and the terror of it haunts his sleep.

He knows there is someone out there who has seen his face when she shouldn't have seen it. He is afraid of her. He tries to alter his appearance as much as he can: he shaves off his moustache and cuts his hair short and spiky. As for the green trousers, he never wears them again. Those trousers, hanging at the back of a wardrobe, the ones he doesn't dare to get rid of in case someone starts asking questions. But he is afraid anyway. And he's afraid that eventually the IOU will turn up, the one he dropped. The one with his name on. He reads the newspaper every day and is terrified that one day he'll read that they have finally found the document, and now at last the murderer will be caught. He is so afraid that over and over again he has to return to the place and search among the bushes, even though he knows it's pointless. He must convince himself that the incriminating piece of paper hasn't got itself trapped among a wilted clump of grass or behind a rock. That's why he sometimes gets in his car and drives the sixty kilometres to that horribly familiar place on the Prairie. Because what was the point of getting a person out of the way to bring an end to the everlasting money worries, only for a stupid piece of paper to ruin everything? He has been playing for high stakes, and he has to finish the game. If he is found out, all will be lost.

Then his wicked deed, which in his own blinkered eyes was unavoidable, will have been the most idiotic, mindless thing he has ever done.

Not once does it occur to him that a person has gone forever—that because of him an old man will never see this summer change into autumn. He only thinks of himself. He will survive whatever the cost. But he is afraid, and a person is never more dangerous than when he is afraid.

The Great Stonytotem hadn't come back from its forensic examination in Stockholm yet, but the police had received proof straight away. Sure enough, the minute quantities of chocolate found on the Great Stonytotem contained traces of arsenic. And what was left of Kalle's bar of chocolate contained almost enough poison to kill someone. If Eva-Lotta had eaten the whole bar, as the sender had hoped, she would have had little chance of survival.

Eva-Lotta knew about the attempt that had been made on her life. It was in every newspaper, so it would have been impossible to keep it from her. Also, the chief inspector thought it was his duty to warn her. The stream of gifts and sweets had stopped, it's true, after the papers had finally stopped urging their readers to send them, but Eva-Lotta needed to be on her guard even so. A desperate person would find other ways to harm her. And even though the chief inspector suspected Eva-Lotta might have another breakdown when she heard the nasty truth, he went to the baker's house anyway to have a serious talk with her.

But he had suspected wrong. Eva-Lotta didn't break down at all. She got so angry, sparks were flying.

'Beppo could have died!' she shouted. 'What kind of person tries to kill a poor innocent dog who had never done anyone any harm?'

In Eva-Lotta's eyes this was the worst outrage she could imagine.

But her carefree nature helped her to forget nasty events. After a few days she was cheerful again. She forgot there were wicked people in the world; she only knew it was the summer holidays and overwhelmingly wonderful to be alive.

Yes, only one miserable little week left of the summer holidays. Every member of the Red and White Roses realized that the short time of freedom that remained must be filled with something better than worrying over things that couldn't be changed.

Beppo was well again, and Sixten, who had been glued to his side, was now filled with a new kind of energy. He called his troops together and they gathered in his garage and forged new plans. Now was the time of revenge, now the Whites would be taught a whopping lesson they'd never forget for putting the Great Stonytotem in the globe, and for all the other tricks they'd got up to. The fact that Anders had poisoned Beppo didn't count—Sixten had forgiven him from the bottom of his heart, and Anders had shown enormous sympathy for Beppo and his sickness.

Battles had raged between the Reds and the Whites even before the Great Stonytotem's time. And even though the Great Stonytotem with all his magical powers was unbeatable as a war trophy, there were other valuable tokens they could steal from each other. The White Roses had a tin box, for example, full of secret documents. Anders felt it was perfectly safe to keep it in the chest of drawers in the bakery loft. And so it was—normally. But now that the Great Stonytotem was away on other business, Sixten came to the conclusion that the White Roses' tin box was an excellent treasure trove that simply had to be seized, even if the Red Roses had to fight to the last man. Benka and Jonte instantly agreed—you couldn't imagine two kids more willing to fight to the last man. Once the heroic decision and solemn oaths had been taken at a meeting in the leader's garage, Sixten went very casually one evening to the Whites' headquarters in the bakery loft, and stole the tin box. The expected outcry from the Whites didn't happen, for the simple reason that they hadn't noticed it was missing. Finally, Sixten's patience ran out and he sent Benka round to the Whites with a letter, to wake them up and make them realize what had happened. The letter said:

Where, White Roses, is your secret box,
And the secrets it contains?

Where the Prairie ends
You'll find a house
And in that house there is a room
And in that room there is a corner
And in that corner is some paper
And on that paper is a map
And on that map... well, can you guess?
Oh, White lice,
Look in that house!

'I will never in my entire life go inside that house again,' said Eva-Lotta.

But on second thoughts she realized she couldn't stay away from the Prairie for the rest of her life. You could play there like nowhere else. The Prairie was always enticing, always full of possibilities. If she could never play on the Prairie again she might as well go and live in a convent.

'I'm coming with you,' she said, after a brief struggle with herself. 'Might as well get it over and done with before I get it all out of proportion.'

The following morning the Whites got up unnaturally early to avoid being taken by surprise by their enemy as they were searching. To be on the safe side, Eva-Lotta didn't tell anyone at home where she was going. She tiptoed through the front gate and joined Anders and Kalle, who had been waiting there for her.

The Prairie wasn't nearly as terrifying as Eva-Lotta had feared. It lay there silent and peaceful as always, with the swallows looping and darting in the air. No, there was nothing to be afraid of here. The Mansion looked almost welcoming, not at all like a sad, abandoned building, but a home where people hadn't quite woken up yet. Soon they might throw open a window, the curtains would flap in the morning breeze, the rooms echo with happy voices, and from the kitchen would come the welcome clatter that meant breakfast. There was certainly nothing to be afraid of here.

But as they stepped through the door it was still only an empty house that received them, a house with spiders' webs in the corners, peeling wallpaper and cracked window panes. The only happy voices here would be their own.

'Oh, White lice, look in that house' the Red leader had challenged them, and they did their best. They had to search for a long time, because it was a big house with many rooms and many hiding places, but finally their search ended in success—just as the Reds had planned. Because now, like never before, the Whites would be properly fooled, so Sixten had decided.

The piece of paper was a map, right enough, and it wasn't difficult to work out that it was the postmaster's garden. There was Sixten's house and the garage and the woodshed and everything, and in one place a circle marked: Dig here!

'I'll say this about the Reds,' said Anders, after he had studied the map for a while. 'They're not exactly imaginative.'

'No, this looks ridiculous,' said Kalle. 'It's so childish, they should be ashamed. But I suppose we'd better get over there and start digging.'

Yes, they would go there and start digging, but first there was something else they wanted to do. Neither Anders or Kalle had been here since that memorable Wednesday. On that occasion they had been turned back by Constable Björk, but now a little twinge of curiosity grabbed them. Shouldn't they go and look at the place after all, while they were here?

'Not me,' said Eva-Lotta emphatically.

She would rather die than walk along that narrow path again. But if Anders and Kalle wanted to, well, good luck to them. She was staying where she was. So long as they came back for her afterwards.

'Yes, we'll be back in ten minutes,' said Kalle.

And off they went.

When Eva-Lotta had been left on her own she began to furnish the house in her imagination, and fill it with a large family with lots of children. Eva-Lotta didn't have any brothers and sisters, and she loved little children.

This is the dining room, Eva-Lotta pretended. Here is

the table. The family is so big, it's a real squash round the table. Krister and Kristina start squabbling and are sent to their bedrooms. Bertil is so young he has to sit in a high chair. His mum feeds him but oh, what a mess he makes! Big sister Liliane is very beautiful. She has black hair and dark eyes, and there will be a ball here this evening. This is the ballroom. She will stand here under the chandelier in a white silk gown, her eyes sparkling.

Eva-Lotta made her own eyes sparkle, and she was big sister Liliane.

Big brother Klas is coming home from university in Uppsala today. He has finished his exams. The father of the family is very glad about that. He stands by the window, looking out and waiting for his son.

Eva-Lotta sticks out her stomach and pretends to be the father, the wealthy owner of the Mansion, standing by the window, waiting for his son.

And look, there he is outside, and he's coming this way! He is very handsome—but he could have been a bit younger!

It took a few seconds for Eva-Lotta to come out of her pretend world and realize that it wasn't big brother Klas striding up towards the mansion, but a real person made of flesh and blood. She laughed at herself in embarrassment—what if she'd called out 'Hello Klas!' to him?

At that moment he looked up and saw her in the

window. He jumped in surprise, did big brother Klas. He didn't look at all happy to see the owner of the house standing there, watching him. All of a sudden he was in a hurry to carry on walking.

A tearing hurry.

Then suddenly he stopped and turned back. Yes, he turned back!

Eva-Lotta thought she wouldn't embarrass him again so she walked into the dining room to see if little Bertil had finished his porridge. He hadn't, so big sister Liliane had to help him. Eva-Lotta was so involved in her game that she didn't hear the door open, and she yelped in surprise when she looked up and saw big brother Klas walking into the room.

'Good morning,' said big brother Klas, or whoever he was.

'Good morning,' said Eva-Lotta.

'I thought I saw a familiar face in here,' said big brother Klas.

'No, it's only me,' said Eva-Lotta.

He looked at her, frowning.

'Haven't we met before, you and me?' he asked.

Eva-Lotta shook her head.

'No, I don't think so,' she said. 'Not that I can remember.'

'I'd pick him out of a thousand other people,' she had

said once. But she didn't know then that a person's appearance could change so fundamentally. A moustache could be shaved off; long, greasy hair could be trimmed short and spiky.

The man she had once collided with on the narrow path, and whose face was forever imprinted in her memory, had been wearing green trousers, and in her mind she couldn't imagine him wearing anything else. Big brother Klas was wearing a grey checked suit.

He looked at her, nervously, and then he asked:

'And what might your name be?'

'Eva-Lotta Lisander.'

Big brother Klas nodded.

'Eva-Lotta Lisander,' he said.

Eva-Lotta hadn't the faintest idea how lucky it was that she didn't recognize big brother Klas. Even a hard-bitten villain will draw the line at harming a child unnecessarily, but this was the man who would stop at nothing to survive. He knew that someone called Eva-Lotta Lisander could ruin everything for him, and he was prepared to do whatever it took to stop that happening. But here she stood, this Eva-Lotta Lisander, who he thought he recognized through the window as soon as he saw her blonde hair. Here she was, saying quite casually that she had never seen him before. The relief he felt was so immense he could have shouted out loud. He didn't have to silence her telltale little mouth that had caused him so much trouble, neither did he have to spend every minute worrying about bumping into Eva-Lotta Lisander if she happened to pop up one day in the town where he lived. She could so easily have pointed at him and said: 'There's the murderer!' But she didn't recognize him, she was no longer a witness, she would never be able to point him out. He was so relieved about this that he was even glad she hadn't been harmed by his murderous attempt with the bar of chocolate that the newspapers had made such a hoo-ha about.

Big brother Klas decided to leave. He would leave and never come back to this hideous place. But even as he stood with his hand on the door handle, he became suspicious. Was she just very clever at acting, this girl, playing the innocent and only pretending she didn't recognize him? He gave her a sidelong glance. But there she stood with her trusting face, smiling and friendly, so it couldn't be an act, he realized that, although otherwise he didn't know that much about honesty. But to be on the safe side he asked:

'What are you doing out here on your own?'

'I'm not on my own,' she said. 'Anders and Kalle are here as well. My friends, you know.'

'So you play out here, do you?' asked big brother Klas.

'Not really,' said Eva-Lotta. 'We've only come here to look for a document.'

'A document?' said big brother Klas, and his look

hardened. 'You've been looking for a document?'

'Yes, for ages,' said Eva-Lotta, who thought an hour was a ridiculously long time to spend looking for the Reds' idiotic map. 'You can't imagine how hard we've looked. But we found it in the end.'

Big brother Klas gasped and gripped the door handle so hard his knuckles turned white.

The game was up, just when he thought he was safe! He felt an insane desire to destroy everything that got in his way. Had he been feeling relieved the kid had survived the poisoned chocolate episode? Well, he wasn't feeling relieved now. All he felt was a cold fury, the kind he had felt that last Wednesday in July.

He forced himself to stay calm. There was still hope. But he had to have that document, he had to!

'So, um, where are Anders and Kalle now?' he asked, as nonchalantly as he could.

'Oh, they'll be here any minute,' said Eva-Lotta.

She looked out of the window.

'Yes, here they come now,' she said.

Big brother Klas stood behind her so he could see for himself. He was standing very close to her, and when she turned her head she happened to look down. And she saw his hand.

She recognized his hand! The memory came back to her. It was a large hand, large and hairy. Thick, black hair. Yes, now she recognized big brother Klas without a doubt.

The fear she felt was so overwhelming that it almost made her faint. The blood drained from her face, only to rush back again the next second with a speed that made her ears ring. It was good she was standing with her back to him, otherwise he would have seen the mad panic in her eyes and her trembling lips as she was about to cry. But at the same time, having him behind her was the worst thing ever, because she didn't know what he was doing. But oh, thank goodness, here were Anders and Kalle! She was not alone in all the world! Those two figures sauntering along in their washed-out jeans, grubby shirts and pitifully uncombed hair, were like a vision from heaven. The knights of the White Roses—what a welcome sight!

But she was also a knight of the White Roses, and as such she must not lose her grip. Her brain was working overtime and surely he could hear it, but one thing she was certain of: he simply mustn't find out that she had recognized him. How she was going to do it, she didn't know, but she had to act naturally.

She opened the window and leaned out. The desperation shone in her eyes, but the two boys outside didn't notice.

'Watch out, they'll be here soon!' shouted Anders, as soon as he saw her.

That made big brother Klas jump. Were the police already on their way to pick up the IOU they had found? Which of the kids had it? He had to get a move on! Time was running out, he had to do something, quick.

He stepped up to the window. He hated coming out into the open, but now he had no choice. He gave the boys a friendly smile.

'Hello there,' he said.

They looked at him, puzzled.

'You shouldn't leave a little lady on her own,' he said, in a voice that was meant to sound jokey, but failed. 'I had to come in here and have a little chat with Eva-Lotta while you were out collecting waste paper, or whatever it was you were doing.'

There was no answer to that, so Anders and Kalle kept quiet, waiting for him to go on.

'Come in, lads,' said the man standing behind Eva-Lotta. 'I have a proposition to put to you. A good proposition that will earn you some money.'

That made Anders and Kalle move fast. If there was money to be earned they wanted to get to the starting line straight away.

But Eva-Lotta was standing at window looking so strangely at them. She made the secret sign of the White Roses, the sign that meant danger. Anders and Kalle stopped in their tracks, confused.

Then Eva-Lotta started singing.

'Here comes the sunshine, here comes the sun...' she began, in a wobbly voice. She continued with the same jolly song, but the words had changed:

'*Mom-u-ror-dod-e-ror-e-ror,*' she sang.

It sounded like one of those nonsense rhymes little children make up, but Anders and Kalle went rigid with horror when they heard it. They stood as if nailed to the spot. Then they pulled themselves together and very casually pinched their ear lobes. That was the White Roses' secret signal for 'understood'.

'Well, hurry up,' the man in the window said, impatiently.

They stood there, hesitating. Then all of a sudden Kalle turned around and headed for some bushes close by.

'Where are you off to?' shouted the man angrily. 'Don't you want to earn some money?'

'Of course I do,' said Kalle. 'But I'm allowed to answer a call of nature first, aren't I?'

The man bit his lip.

'Make it snappy, then,' he said.

'Oh yes, I'll hurry,' said Kalle.

It took a while but eventually he returned, demonstratively buttoning his trousers. Anders was standing in the same place as before. There wasn't the slightest chance he would leave Eva-Lotta in her time of need. He had to go to her, into that house where the murderer was, but he would rather go in with Kalle by his side.

So in they went, into the ballroom where big sister Liliane would be dancing that evening. Anders walked over to Eva-Lotta and put his arm round her shoulder.

He looked at her watch and exclaimed:

'Rats, look at the time! We've got to head for home right away.'

He grabbed Eva-Lotta's hand and ran to the door.

'Yes, we'll have to earn that money another day,' said Kalle. 'Got to be off!'

But if they thought big brother Klas was going to swallow that, they were mistaken. Suddenly he was there in front of them, blocking the doorway.

'Slow down, kids,' he said. 'You're not in that much of a rush, surely?'

He felt in his back pocket. Yes, it was there. Ever since that last Wednesday in July he had always carried it with him, to cover any eventualities.

The thoughts raced in his head. Fear and rage made him lose all common sense. Yes, there was fear because of what he had to do, but he felt no hesitation. He had played for high stakes, and he had to see the game through to the end, even if it cost another couple of lives.

He looked at the three children in front of him, and he hated them for what he had to do. But he had to do it. He couldn't have three witnesses who could tell others what the man looked like, the man who had forced them to hand over the IOU. No, they would never have the opportunity to tell. He regretted it, and his stomach lurched in fear. But first he had to know which of them had the document, so that he wouldn't have to search through their pockets—afterwards.

'Listen to me,' he said, his voice sounding hoarse. 'That document you found a minute ago—give it here. Quick!'

The three children in front of him gasped in astonishment. They could not have been more surprised if he'd opened his mouth and started singing 'Baa Baa Black Sheep'. Could they believe their ears? They'd heard about murderers who were nothing less than insane, but not a crackpot who could find any use for the Red Roses' map with the order 'Dig here!'

But why not? Let him have the map, if it was so important to him, thought Anders, who had the piece of paper in his pocket.

In a critical situation, it was always Master Detective Kalle Blomkvist who thought the fastest. In a split second he realized exactly what kind of document the murderer thought they had. And quite a lot else became clear to him at the same time. It was as if he could read the man's thoughts. This creep had cold-bloodedly shot a man to death, and it was highly likely he was armed now. He had tried to get the witness Eva-Lotta out of the way with poisoned chocolate. Kalle realized the chances of them getting out of here alive were very small. Even if Anders fished that paper out of his pocket, and they managed to convince the killer they'd never caught so much as a glimpse of his IOU, they were still done for.

The murderer must have understood that his question had revealed everything, and Kalle knew that if he had tried to get rid of one witness, he certainly wasn't going to allow three to wander around freely, liable to identify him. Kalle didn't formulate this in words, it was only an awareness in his brain, an awareness that made him feel faint with terror. But he said angrily to himself: You can be afraid afterwards—if there is going to be an 'afterwards'.

What was important now was to gain time. Oh, how they had to gain time!

Anders was just about to take the map out of his pocket when Kalle nudged him hard.

'Non-o,' hissed Kalle. 'Dod-o-non-tot!'

'Didn't you hear me?' demanded big brother Klas. 'Who's got the document?'

'We haven't got it here,' said Kalle.

Anders thought it would have been better to hand the document over and then they might be allowed to go. But he knew Kalle had more experience of dealing with criminal types, so he kept quiet.

The man by the door exploded with anger when he heard Kalle's words.

'Where have you put it?' he screamed. 'Get it now— quick!'

Kalle was thinking as fast as he could. If he said the document was at the police station, or at Eva-Lotta's house, or out on the Prairie somewhere, they would never get away with it. He knew they were safe only for as long as the murderer still had some hope of getting his hands on the document quickly.

'We put it upstairs,' he said, speaking deliberately slowly.

By this time big brother Klas was so furious he was shaking all over. He took his pistol out of his back pocket and Eva-Lotta closed her eyes.

'March!' he shrieked. 'Maybe this will help your legs go faster.'

And he drove them in front of him, out of the room where big sister Liliane would be dancing that evening.

'Gog-o sos-lol-o-wow-lol-yoy,' said Kalle under his breath. 'Pop-o-lol-i-coc-e o-non tot-hoh-e wow-a-yoy.'

Anders and Eva-Lotta looked at him in amazement. How come the police were on their way? Did he think he could get them here by some kind of telepathy? But they obeyed his instruction to go slowly. They dragged their feet, they tripped over doorsteps, and Anders staggered and fell backwards down the staircase, just like he had done a million years ago, when they were battling the Reds on this very spot.

Their dawdling made big brother Klas absolutely beside himself with rage. He was so close to the limit of what he could tolerate that he was almost tempted to do it now—the thing he was going to do. But he had to have the IOU first. Oh, these kids, how he hated them! They didn't even seem to know which corner they'd hidden it in. They went at a snail's pace from one room to another, saying distractedly: 'No, not here.'

It would have been easier to steer a rampaging herd of cattle. These blasted kids stopped to blow their noses, scratch themselves, have a cry—it was mostly the girl who cried, of course.

Eventually they came to a small room with ancient flaking wallpaper. Eva-Lotta sniffed loudly as she remembered how she and Kalle had been locked in here once, when they were still young and happy.

Kalle surveyed the walls.

'No, I don't think it was here,' he said.

'Nope, definitely not here,' said Anders.

But this was the last of the upstairs rooms, and big brother Klas let out a strangled cry.

'Don't think you can fool me!' he shouted. 'Don't you think I know what you're up to? So just you listen to me. You're going to find that piece of paper, and I mean now. At once. And if you've forgotten where it is, so much the worse for you. If I don't get that document in five seconds, I'll shoot you, all three of you.'

He stood with his back to the window, aiming the pistol at them.

Kalle realized he meant what he said, and that their tactic wouldn't work any longer. He nodded at Anders.

Anders walked over to the wall. He raised his hand, which he had been keeping in his trouser pocket, and put it behind a piece of peeling wallpaper. When he took it out again he was clutching a piece of paper.

'Here it is,' he said,

'Good,' said big brother Klas. 'Stand close together, the three of you. Now, hand me the document.'

'Gog-e-tot dod-o-wow-non o-non tot-hoh-e fof-lol-o-o-ror wow-hoh-e-non I sos-non-e-e-zoz-e,' said Kalle.

Anders and Eva-Lotta touched their earlobes to indicate they had understood.

Big brother Klas heard one of the youngsters utter what he thought was a kind of terrified gobbledygook, but what it meant didn't interest him. He knew this would soon be over. As soon as he had the document he would do it.

He reached out and took the piece of paper Anders was holding out to him, all the time keeping his pistol aimed. But his fingers shook as he tried to unfold the document with only one hand.

IOU? What IOU? 'Dig here'—that's not what an IOU normally said! His brain froze for exactly half a second, and that's when Kalle sneezed violently.

Simultaneously, the three youngsters threw themselves to the floor. Kalle and Anders lurched forward and grabbed Klas's legs. He fell headlong, yelling as he hit the floor. The pistol bounced out of his hand and

Kalle picked it up a split second before their opponent could grab it again.

This, then, was one of those occasions when Master Detective Blomkvist disarmed a murderer. He was used to doing it, of course, and always with such elegance. And as usual he turned the pistol on the criminal and said: 'Not so fast, my good man.'

Was that what he said this time? No, it wasn't. In utter panic he gripped the hateful black object and threw it out of the window, sending shards of glass flying everywhere. That's what he did. It was hardly a well-thought-out plan of action for a master detective. It would have been handy to have a pistol right now. But to tell the truth, Master Detective Blomkvist was scared to death by all weapons, apart from his own catapult, that is. And perhaps he did the right thing, after all. A pistol in the hand of a trembling boy is no real threat to a desperate murderer. The roles would quickly have been reversed. That's why it was best the pistol was out of reach for both of them. Big brother Klas rushed to the window and looked in confusion and anger in the direction his pistol had taken. This was his biggest and most serious mistake, and the three White Roses didn't waste any time turning it to their advantage. They headed for the door at top speed. The only door in the house that could be locked, as they knew from bitter experience.

Big brother Klas was hot on their heels, but they got

out just in time and three strong feet were held against the door while Kalle turned the key. They heard a bellowing from inside, and a wild thumping on the door. To be on the safe side, Kalle took out the key, just in case big brother Klas happened to be familiar with the trick of opening a locked door from the inside.

They clattered down the ancient, graceful staircase, gasping with anxiety and shaking all over.

All three squeezed through the front door at the same time, hardly knowing where they were running. But Kalle said, practically in tears:

'We've got to get the pistol.'

The murder weapon had to be recovered, he knew that. But the very moment they turned the corner of the Mansion it happened. Something came hurtling out through the open window and landed right in front of them. Big brother Klas had jumped. It was a drop of five metres, but he was far too desperate to let a minor detail like that stand in his way. He survived the jump, and he had found the revolver. This time he wouldn't talk, he would act.

The three children had retreated around the corner of the house in the brief moment it had taken for him to pick up the pistol. But just wait! It would be their turn soon! Any minute he would...

Then he heard the sound of a voice crying and cheering at the same time. It was the girl.

'The police! Over there! They're coming! Oh, quick, quick! Constable Björk, hurry!'

He looked out across the Prairie. Yes, hell and damnation, here they came, a whole mob of them!

It was too late to do anything to the children now, but perhaps not too late to run away. He snivelled in fear. Yes, he had to run away. Run to the car. Throw himself inside and drive away like a lunatic, far away, to another country!

He ran to where he had parked the car, pushing himself to the limit because the police were coming closer, sprinting towards him, just the way they did in his nightmares.

But they wouldn't get him. He had a good start and if only he could reach the car then they could try all they wanted. There it was, his lovely, precious little car. He was saved! He felt wildly triumphant as he frantically raced the last few metres. He was going to get away with it. Hadn't he said that all along?

He put the key in the ignition and started the engine. Goodbye, everyone who thought they could stop him. Goodbye forever!

But his car, his lovely, precious car that usually motored along so fast and so smoothly, now jolted and bumped itself forwards agonisingly slowly. He swore between gritted teeth and cried out in rage. When he looked out of the window he saw why: all four tyres had a puncture!

His pursuers were gaining on him, cautiously but determined. They assumed he was armed and they took cover behind bushes and rocks, running in a zigzag pattern. But they were closing in.

He hurled himself out of the car. He could have fired his pistol at them, but he didn't. They would get him anyway, he knew that now.

A short distance away was some dense undergrowth and right behind it a pond which, despite the heat of the summer, was full of stagnant water. He knew it well, the number of times he'd been here before. He ran towards it, and down into its slimy water he threw the pistol. Now no one could find the murder weapon and use it as evidence against him.

Then he ran back to the road in a wide curve, and there he stopped and waited. He was ready now. They could come and get him.

16

The chief inspector leaned forward in his chair and fixed his eyes on the pale young man. It was because of him the chief inspector had been forced to make a very speedy return to the little town.

'Wouldn't it be better to confess?' he said kindly. 'We know you shot Gren. We know you sent that chocolate to Eva-Lotta Lisander. Wouldn't it be nice to put an end to this long interrogation and tell me all about it?'

But the young man repeated arrogantly that he had nothing whatsoever to do with the murder of Gren, that he didn't even know he who he was, and it certainly wasn't him who sent the chocolate to Eva-Lotta Lisander.

The chief inspector asked him yet again why he had tried to flee when the police came out to the Prairie. If he'd had nothing to hide, that is.

The young man got very irritated when he had to explain it again. He had run because the kids were screaming their heads off, he said. Like he had been trying to hurt them. Obviously they had completely misunderstood he was only pretending. Yes, it was stupid of him to run away, but surely the chief inspector knew how sensitive it was, being accused of harming children. And anyway, he had soon stopped running and waited for the police. Maybe it was a stupid game he had played with the children, he couldn't deny that. The little girl had told him about a piece of paper they had found, a map, and he thought it would be fun to frighten them a bit. Pretend he was an enemy who wanted the map, so he could join in the hunt for the buried treasure. The chief inspector had seen the map himself, so he knew he wasn't lying. It was true what the children said, that he had pointed a pistol at them, but have a heart, Inspector, the pistol wasn't loaded!

Where was the pistol now, the inspector wanted to know.

Yes, that's exactly what the young man wanted to know as well. It was a good pistol, left to him by his father. But one of the kids had chucked it out of a window—honestly, they took it so seriously, it made you laugh!—and since then he hadn't seen any trace of the weapon. Some other blasted kid must have taken it, no doubt the same one who slashed his tyres.

The chief inspector shook his head.

'You're a very good liar, lad,' he said. 'But don't forget one thing. Eva-Lotta Lisander is convinced you are the man she met on the Prairie a couple of minutes after Gren was shot.'

The young man gave a superior laugh.

'Strange, very strange,' he said. 'So how come she was chatting to me like we were the best of friends, telling me about that map and her mates and I don't know what else. She must think murderers are nice people.'

The inspector was quiet for a moment, but then he said:

'Your landlady told us you shaved off your moustache recently. The day after the murder, to be precise. Why was that?'

The young man looked at the inspector's clean-shaven face.

'Have you never grown a little moustache just for fun, and then shaved it off when you got tired of it? And can I help it if the poor old geezer got shot the day before I did it?'

'I see,' said the inspector. 'Then I should perhaps tell you that we searched your rooms yesterday and found a pair of dark-green trousers hanging at the back of your wardrobe. You are perhaps aware that for the past fourteen days the police have been looking for a man with dark-green trousers?'

The young man sitting opposite him turned a shade paler, but he still sounded arrogant when he said:

'I guarantee you that at least five of my mates have got

green trousers. And that's not a punishable offence, as far as I've heard.'

The inspector shook his head again.

'Lad,' he said. 'I don't know how you've got the energy to keep this up.'

But the young man did have the energy. He had the energy to lie for so long that the inspector nearly his patience, and he was known for his patience throughout the entire police force. Big brother Klas was made of tough stuff—and yes, by a strange twist of fate Klas actually was his real name. Eva-Lotta's choice had been the right one.

The dramatic events at the Mansion had badly disrupted the Wars of the Roses. Yet again, everyone's mum was gripped by fear, yet again the children were under strict instructions to stay at home. But in fact they were so affected by what had happened, they really didn't feel like doing anything at all. The Reds and the Whites sat together in the baker's garden, going over the horrific minutes out on the Prairie. Kalle was praised again for his quick thinking, because it certainly had been clever of him to make up that story about needing to answer a call of nature. He knew the Reds were closing in on them—he and Anders had seen them sneaking around the bushes—so he ran to them as fast as he could and gave them a quick, urgent order: 'The murderer's at the Mansion. Run and get the police! And his car's parked by the bend in the road—one of you go and slash his tyres!'

After the interrogation of big brother Klas had gone on for another twenty-four hours, give or take a few short breaks, and the inspector's patience had been stretched almost to the limit, Benka happened to be at home one rainy afternoon, looking at his stamp collection. In reality Benka was a fairly quiet child, and not especially keen on fighting, but he had an idol who was made of sterner stuff, one he followed through thick and thin. That idol was Sixten. And with Sixten's influence Benka had become a useful member of the Red Roses. However, on a rainy afternoon like this you could sit peacefully indoors and sort out your stamp collection without a guilty conscience. He was a bit short-sighted so he leaned in closer to peer fondly at his stamps. He had an almost complete collection of Swedish stamps and was about to stick in some he had only recently got hold of when he caught sight of a crumpled envelope. Oh yes, that was the one he had found on the street outside the Lisander's house a while ago. It had a brand new stamp from the latest issue on it, and that's why Benka had picked it up from the gutter. He had never seen one of those stamps before.

He smoothed out the envelope. He hadn't done that

earlier—all he had done was chuck it into the box where he kept the stamps still waiting to be removed from their envelopes.

'Miss Eva-Lotta Lisander' was typed on the front. That girl had certainly been getting a lot of post recently! He peered inside the envelope. Empty, naturally! He looked at the stamp again, and it made him happy when he saw it was a particularly beautiful one. He couldn't tell from the post mark where it had come from, but the date was clear.

And suddenly a thought struck him like a flash of lightning! What if this was the envelope everyone was making such a fuss about? The one the police had spent ages looking for? Let's think. The day the Whites were sitting among the lilacs in the baker's garden, and Sixten had sent him to annoy them—wasn't that the day the chocolate arrived? Crikey, it was! And that was when he had found the envelope. What a corking great twerp he was not to have taken a closer look at it!

It took him two minutes to run through the rain to Sixten, who was at home playing chess with Jonte. Then it took them two minutes to run to Eva-Lotta, who was up in the bakery loft with Anders and Kalle, reading comics and listening to the rain drumming on the roof. And it took all of them two minutes to hurtle down to the police station. It took ten minutes, however, for the soaking wet group to explain to Constable Björk and the chief inspector why they had come.

The chief inspector studied the envelope through a magnifying glass. There was clearly something wrong with the 't' key on this typewriter—a little spike stuck out on one side of every letter 't'.

'Kids are like dogs,' said the chief inspector later. 'They nose around all over the place and dig up a lot of rubbish, but all of a sudden they bring home something worth having.'

The envelope turned out to be extremely worth having. True enough, big brother Klas had a typewriter, and when it was proved that the letter 't' on his machine had exactly the same fault as the 't' on the envelope, the chief inspector felt it was high time to bring a charge.

But the man they had arrested still stubbornly refused to admit his guilt. The police would have to charge him on evidence alone.

Sixten had made another map with 'Dig here' on it. One warm evening he brought it round to the White Roses, who had gathered in the bakery garden.

'"Dig here",' Anders said, when Sixten shoved the map into his hand. 'That's easy for you to say. Your dad will go mad when we come over and start making a mess of his front lawn.'

'Who said anything about a lawn?' replied Sixten.

'Follow the map and I guarantee you Dad won't go mad. Benka, Jonte and me are off swimming now. See you later.'

The Whites trooped off to the postmaster's garden. They took measurements and paced out distances and compared them with the map, and finally they came to the conclusion that the tin box was buried in an overgrown strawberry bed. They began digging away happily, and every time a spade hit a stone they gave a loud cheer, thinking it was the box. But they were disappointed every time, and went back to digging frenetically. After working their way through practically the entire strawberry bed, Kalle burst out:

'Here it is, at last!'

He scrabbled about with his fingers and lifted out the box, which was covered in earth. Craftily it had been buried in the very farthest corner. Anders and Eva-Lotta threw down their spades and rushed over. Eva-Lotta gently wiped their precious trophy box clean with her handkerchief, and Anders took the key from around his neck, where he always kept it. The box felt worryingly light. What if the Reds had somehow got hold of another key and made off with their trophies? They opened the box fast, to find out.

But inside there were no secret documents or trophies of any kind. There was only one sheet of paper, written in Sixten's revolting handwriting, and it was a challenge:

Keep on digging, don't stop now!
Only a few thousand miles to go
and you'll reach New Zealand.
Why don't you stay there!

The Whites howled in exasperation, and from behind the hedge came an explosion of laughter. Out came Sixten, Benka and Jonte.

'You vermin! What have you done with our stash of treasure?' shrieked Anders.

Sixten slapped his leg and laughed for a long time before he answered.

'You oaf,' he said. 'Do you think we're interested in your stupid old relics? They're still there, among all the rest of the junk in your chest of drawers. You're not paying attention, are you?'

'No, all you're doing is digging,' said Jonte smugly.

'Yes, you're very good at digging,' said Sixten. 'Dad's going to be thrilled. He's been nagging at me to dig over this strawberry bed for ages. I've not been too keen, in this heat.'

'I can believe that, the way you dug for the Great Stonytotem,' said Kalle. 'You've probably still got the blisters.'

'You'll pay for this,' said Anders.

'You can say that again,' said Eva-Lotta. She shook the earth from her handkerchief and put it back in her pocket. Hang on, there was something else in there, right at the bottom. She pulled it out and had a look at it. 'IOU' it said at the top. Eva-Lotta chuckled.

'You'll never guess what,' she said. 'Here's that old IOU. It's been in my wardrobe all the time, while people have been swarming all over the Prairie looking for it. It's true what I've said all along. There's something incredibly stupid about IOUs.'

She took a closer look at the document.

'Klas,' she said. 'Well, the name's right. And his signature's very neat, by the way.'

Then she crumpled up the IOU and tossed it across the lawn, where it was picked up by a light summer breeze.

'Oh well, the police have got him now,' she said. 'So it doesn't matter what his signature looks like.'

Kalle yelled and threw himself after the priceless document. He looked disapprovingly at Eva-Lotta.

'I'll tell you this, Eva-Lotta,' he said. 'Things are going to end badly for you if you don't stop throwing bits of paper about like this.'

17

'Lol-o-non-gog lol-i-vov-e tot-hoh-e Ror-e-dod Ror-o-sos-e-sos,' said Sixten, with some effort. 'A ridiculously easy language, when you think about it.'

'Oh yes, now you know the key to the code,' said Anders.

'And anyway, you've got to say it faster,' said Kalle.

'Yes, it isn't supposed to be one word today and one tomorrow,' said Eva-Lotta. 'You've got to go rat-a-tat-tat, like a machine gun.'

They were sitting all together in the bakery loft, the knights of the Red and the White Roses, and the Reds had just had their first lesson in the Robber language. When they thought about it, the Whites realized it was their civic duty to introduce the Reds to the secrets of the language. The value of learning a language cannot be overstated, that's what they were told in school. And how right that was! Otherwise how would Kalle and Anders and Eva-Lotta have survived the events at the Mansion if they hadn't been able to use their Robber language? Kalle had been thinking about that for a few days, and eventually he said to Anders and Eva-Lotta:

'We can't let the Reds walk around in such stonking ignorance. If they happen to bump into a murderer it'll be an absolute shambles.'

That's why the Whites had started giving language lessons in the bakery loft. Sixten had a whacking great Fail in English and should have been cramming English grammar from morning to night, seeing as he was going to have a test on it any day. But he considered it more important to spend his time learning how to speak the Robber language.

'Every murderer knows English,' he said. 'So that won't help us much. But without the Robber language we're sunk.'

And as a result he and Benka and Jonte sat for hours in the bakery loft, practising with a touching enthusiasm.

The language lesson was interrupted by the baker, who came climbing up the stairs from the bakery. He was carrying a plate of freshly-baked cinnamon buns, which he handed to Eva-Lotta, saying:

'Constable Björk has just phoned. He says the Great Stonytotem has come back.'

'Gog-o-o-dod!' said Eva-Lotta, overjoyed, and helped herself to a bun. 'Come on, let's get down to the police station!'

'Gog-o-o-dod indeed,' said the baker. 'But take it easy with that Great Stonytotem in future, will you?'

Oh yes, the knights of the Red and the White Roses promised the baker that of course they would take it easy, ha ha! And with that the baker went downstairs.

'Oh, and by the way, that bloke Klas has confessed at last,' he said, before he disappeared.

Yes, big brother Klas had confessed. There was no denying the evidence now, thanks to the IOU.

So here it was, the moment he had thought about with such terror, the moment that had tormented him during so many restless nights. The moment his guilt would be proved and he would have to take responsibility for what he had done.

Big brother Klas had not felt at peace for many years. The constant need for money that had driven him into shady deals with Gren, had turned him into a restless, hunted person, who couldn't find a moment's peace. And after that terrible Wednesday at the end of July his anxiety had grown into an unbearable terror, which wouldn't leave him, night or day.

How must he be feeling now, when he had to openly admit to his crime and be prepared to pay for it for many years to come? Surely now, like never before, the anxiety must be crushing him.

No—it was strange. Big brother Klas was calmer than

he had been for years. A huge feeling of peace came over him after he had admitted everything. He had never felt anything like it before. He wept for a while over his weakness, and his own hand trembled as he gripped the chief inspector's strong, safe hand, as if he was looking for comfort. But he wasn't feeling anxious any more, and he fell into a deep, dreamless sleep, that for a short while let him forget the wrong he had done.

He was sleeping when the White and Red Roses came charging into the police station to collect the Great Stonytotem. He didn't hear their eager voices as they crowded into Constable Björk's office to ask for the trophy to be returned.

'The Great Stonytotem,' Constable Bjork said slowly. 'The Great Stonytotem isn't here.'

They stared at him, flabbergasted. What did he mean? He was the one who had phoned to say it had come back.

Constable Bjork looked at them gravely.

'Seek high above the earth,' he said in an impressive voice. 'Let the birds of heaven show you the way. Ask the ravens if they have seen the esteemed Great Stonytotem!'

A smile of comprehension spread over the faces of the Roses. Jonte said, with a chuckle:

'Gog-o-o-dod! The battle continues!'

'The battle continues,' said Benka firmly.

Eva-Lotta looked at Constable Bjork fondly as he sat there looking so handsome in his uniform, trying to look serious.

'Constable Bjork,' she said. 'If you weren't so incredibly old, you could join us in the Wars of the Roses.'

'Yes, Constable Bjork could be a Red Rose,' said Sixten.

'Not likely,' said Anders. 'White!'

'By Jove,' said Constable Bjork. 'I wouldn't dare get involved in such dangerous activities. The calm, secure job of a police officer—that's what suits an old chap like me.'

'Tosh. You've got to live dangerously sometimes,' said Kalle.

A couple of hours later he was stretched out in his favourite place under the pear tree, thinking about that living dangerously lark. As he thought, he stared so intently into the summer sky that he scarcely noticed his imaginary listener come creeping up beside him.

'I hear that Mr Blomkvist has yet again managed to nab a murderer,' he said, flatteringly.

Rage suddenly bubbled up inside Kalle Blomkvist.

'Oh, have I?' he said, glaring angrily at the imaginary listener, who wouldn't leave him in peace. 'Don't talk such a lot of twaddle! I haven't caught a murderer. The police have, because that's their job. I don't plan on catching a murderer ever, in my entire life. I intend to stop dabbling in all that crime business now. It only lands you in a lot of trouble.'

'But I thought Mr Blomkvist liked living dangerously,' said the imaginary listener, and to be honest he sounded as if he was giving Kalle a ticking off.

'As if I don't live dangerously enough anyway,' said the master detective. 'Young man, if only you knew what went on in the Wars of the Roses!'

His thoughts were rudely interrupted by the crack of a hard apple core hitting his head. The clever master detective quickly worked out that an apple core doesn't usually fall from a pear tree, and he looked around for the culprit.

Anders and Eva-Lotta were standing over by the fence.

'Wake up, sleepyhead,' called Anders. 'We're off to hunt for the Great Stonytotem.'

'And do you know what we think?' said Eva-Lotta. 'We think Constable Bjork has hidden it in the observation tower in the park. You know how many rooks there are there!'

'Gog-ror-e-a-tot!' shouted Kalle, excitedly.

'The Reds will beat us to a pulp if we find it first,' said Anders.

'Who cares?' said Kalle. 'You've got to live dangerously from time to time.'

Kalle looked meaningfully at his imaginary listener— did he get it now? That you could live dangerously without being a master detective? Discreetly he said goodbye to the nice young man who stood there watching him leave, with more admiration in his eyes than ever.

Kalle's bare brown feet hammered against the garden path as he ran out to Anders and Eva-Lotta. His imaginary listener had gone, and he stayed gone. He had disappeared very quietly and unnoticed, as if carried off by the light summer breeze.

ALSO BY ASTRID LINDGREN

Astrid Lindgren

Astrid Lindgren (1907-2002) is one of the most widely-read children's authors in the world. In the course of her life she wrote over 80 books for children, and has sold over 160 million copies worldwide. She once commented, 'I write to amuse the child within me, and can only hope that other children may have some fun that way too'.

Many of Astrid Lindgren's stories are based upon her memories of childhood and they are filled with lively and unconventional characters. Perhaps the best known is *Pippi Longstocking*, first published in Sweden in 1945. It was an immediate success, and was published in England in 1954.

Awards for Astrid Lindgren's writing include the prestigious Hans Christian Andersen Award and the International Book Award. In 1989 a theme park dedicated to her—*Astrid Lindgren Varld*—was opened in her home town of Vimmerby. When she passed away in 2002, the Swedish Government founded The Astrid Lindgren Memorial Award (ALMA) in her honour. It is the world's largest prize for children's and young adult literature.

FOLLOW KALLE BLOMKVIST IN HIS OTHER EXCITING ADVENTURES...

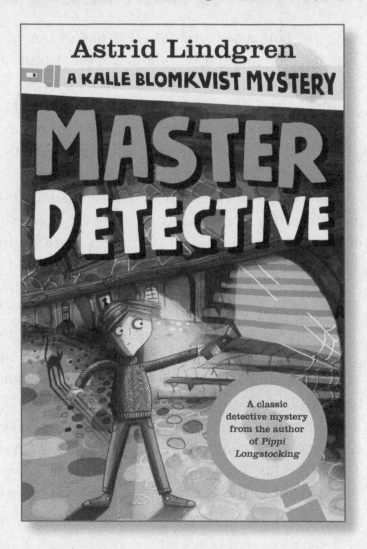

When a mysterious stranger arrives in town, Kalle finds the perfect excuse to start an investigation, one that will draw him and his friends into a thrilling case of theft and deception.

TURN THE PAGE TO READ AN EXTRACT.

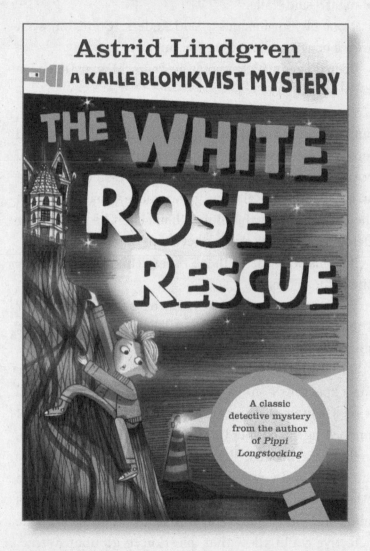

Astrid Lindgren

A KALLE BLOMKVIST MYSTERY

THE WHITE ROSE RESCUE

A classic detective mystery from the author of *Pippi Longstocking*

When Kalle Blomkvist becomes an eye witness to a mysterious kidnapping he doesn't hesitate to take on the case, one which becomes his most dangerous and challenging yet.

'Who the heck would be driving out here at this time of night?' said Kalle.

'None of your business,' said Anders. 'Come on, what are we hanging about here for, anyway?'

Deep down in Kalle's soul the sleepy Master Detective stirred.

There were times when Kalle wasn't Kalle at all, but Master Detective Blomkvist, the brilliant and unstoppable protector of public safety, who divided people into two main categories: 'arrested' and 'not arrested yet'. But Kalle had grown more sensible through the years and now the times when he felt he was Master Detective were few and far between.

But this was one of those times. This was absolutely one of those times.

The person driving that car, where was he heading? There was only one house up here, Eklund House, standing like a solitary outpost far above the town's other buildings. It didn't look as if the professor inside was expecting visitors—the house was sleeping. Could it be a couple in the car, coming up here for a bit of smooching? A couple totally unfamiliar with the area, in that case, because the usual place was in the opposite direction, and you would have to be potty about each other to drive up this winding, hilly road for a bit of smooching in the dark. So who is it in the car? No true detective could allow that question to go unanswered.

It was quite impossible.

'Can't we wait a minute to see who it is?' said Kalle.

'Why?' asked Eva-Lotta. 'Do you think it's a midnight murderer on the loose?'

She had hardly finished speaking before two men appeared by the front gate of Eklund House, no more that twenty-five metres away. They could hear the gate squeak softly on its hinges as the two opened it slowly and walked in. Yes, they walked in!

'Get down in the ditch!' Kalle whispered suddenly, and the next second they were sitting with their noses poking over the top of the ditch, just enough to see what was happening in the professor's garden.

'Well, I expect the professor has invited them,' whispered Anders.

'That's what you think,' said Kalle.

If these really were guests of the professor, they were acting very strangely indeed. If you are someone's guest you don't sneak around as if you are afraid of being discovered. You don't walk round and round the house, you don't test the doors and windows. A welcome guest who finds the house locked doesn't put a ladder under an open window and climb in that way.

But that was what these two night visitors were doing.

'I think I'm going to die,' panted Eva-Lotta. 'Look, they're actually climbing in!'

And that's exactly what the visitors were doing, no

doubt about it, if they could believe what their eyes were telling them.

They lay there in the ditch, staring anxiously at the open window and the flapping curtain. An eternity passed. An eternity of silence with no other sounds except their worried breathing and the soft rustle of the dawn breeze in the cherry trees.

Eventually one of the two visitors came out onto the ladder again. He was carrying something in his arms. What on earth was it?

'Rasmus,' whispered Eva-Lotta, and her face turned pale. 'Look, they're kidnapping Rasmus.'

No, that wasn't possible, thought Kalle. Things like that simply didn't happen. Not here. In America, maybe—he had read about it in the papers—but not here.

Apparently it could happen here. It really was Rasmus the man was carrying. He was holding him gently in his arms, and Rasmus was sleeping.

When the man and his burden had disappeared through the gate, Eva-Lotta burst into tears. She turned her deathly pale face to Kalle and whimpered, like she had when Anders was hanging in the bush:

'What shall we do, Kalle? What shall we do?'

Kalle was far too shaken to give a sensible answer. He ran his fingers nervously through his hair and stuttered:

'I don't know... We... we've got get Constable Björk... We've got to...'

He struggled fiercely to overcome the awful paralysis that stopped him thinking clearly. Something had to be done, and fast. But he wasn't able to work out what that could be. They would never have time to fetch the police, he could work that out for himself, at least. The villains would have time to kidnap a dozen kids before the police arrived, and anyway...

The man who had taken Rasmus was coming back. But now he wasn't carrying Rasmus. 'Left him in the car, of course,' whispered Anders.

Eva-Lotta answered with a muffled sob.

They watched the movements of the kidnapper, wide-eyed. To think there could be such despicable people... the swine!

The veranda door opened and the man's accomplice came into sight.

'Get a move on, Nick,' he called on a low voice, 'We've got to get this over and done with as quick as we can.'

In a few strides the man called Nick was on the veranda, and they both disappeared into the house.

Kalle sprang to life.

'Come on,' he said, nervously. 'We've got to kidnap Rasmus back!'

'If there's time,' said Anders.

'Yes, if there's time,' agreed Kalle. 'Where do you think the car is?'

It was parked nearby, on the top of the hill. They

rushed over to it, running along the ditch as quietly as they could, and they felt incredibly triumphant at the thought of rescuing Rasmus from the hands of the villains. Incredibly triumphant and incredibly afraid.

At the very last second they noticed someone was keeping a watch on the car. There was a man standing on the other side of the road. But as luck would have it he turned his back to them for a moment, and quick as lightning they were able to hurl themselves behind some bushes. They were just in time. The man must have heard a sound that alarmed him, because he whipped round and crossed over to their side of the road. He stood there, staring suspiciously right at the bushes where they were hiding. Could he really not hear their hammering hearts and panting breath?

It seemed a miracle that he couldn't. He stood and listened for a while, then walked round the car and looked in through a side window. Then he paced nervously up and down the road. He came to a halt from time to time and stared towards the house. Perhaps he thought his partners were taking too long?

But there was despair behind the bushes. What could they do while that man was walking about out there? Eva-Lotta cried and Kalle had to nudge her roughly to make her shut up, and also because it wasn't helping his own anxiety.

'Jeepers,' said Anders. 'What are we going to do?'

Then Eva-Lotta swallowed a sob and said briskly:

'I've got to get to Rasmus in the car. If he's going to be kidnapped, so am I. He's not going to face a load of kidnappers on his own when he wakes up.'

'Yes, but...'

'Don't talk,' said Eva-Lotta. 'Go and make a suspicious noise in that bush over there, so he forgets the car for a while.'

Anders and Kalle looked at her in horror, but they saw she had made up her mind. And when Eva-Lotta made up her mind, they knew from experience that nothing would change it.

'Let me do it instead,' begged Kalle, but he knew already it was a waste of time.

'Go!' said Eva-Lotta. 'And hurry up!'

They did as she told them, but before they disappeared they heard her whisper behind them:

'I'll be like a mum to Rasmus. And I'll leave a trail after me, if I can. You know, like Hansel and Gretel.'

'Good,' said Kalle. 'And we'll follow you like two bloodhounds.'

They gave her a wave of encouragement and tore off silently through the bushes.

How good it is on occasions like this to have a gift for creeping about silently! Not for nothing had they been taking part in their Wars of the Roses for such a long time. They'd had plenty of practice in capturing lookout positions. Like that oaf on the road, for example! He was supposed to be keeping an eye on Rasmus, those were his orders. But here he is, pacing up and down between the car and the house. Up and down, up and down. And then he hears a suspicious crackling in that bush over there, and of course he has to go and investigate. He leaps over the ditch and plunges into the tangle of hazel bushes. Oh yes, very much on his guard and very watchful! But it was the car he should have been guarding, the buffoon! All sorts of things could be going on at the car while he's investigating the hazel bushes. A complete waste of time! He finds nothing there, nothing at all. In actual fact there are two boys in there, curled under a bush, but he doesn't see them. And he is stupid enough to think he was imagining things, or that perhaps it was only an animal in the undergrowth. He feels he's very good at what he does, and he's proved that now. And he is very pleased with himself as he returns to the car.

And here they come at last, his partners. The two spies crawling out from the undergrowth see them as well.

'Look, it's the professor,' whispers Kalle. 'They're kidnapping him too!'

Is it true? Or is it only a bad dream? Is that really the professor they are frogmarching towards the car? A wildly resisting, furious, desperate professor, with his hands tied behind his back and a gag over his mouth?

It is nightmarish and dreadful, but it isn't a dream. It's

starting to get light now, and everything can be seen in awful clarity. The dust the professor's feet are kicking up as he struggles is not a dream. The car door slamming behind him is also horribly real. Now the car races down the hill and disappears. The road stands empty in the dawn light. It could have been a bad dream, all of it, if it wasn't for the faint smell of petrol in the air. And if wasn't for a small, wet handkerchief lying on the roadside. Eva-Lotta's handkerchief.

Ready for more great stories?
Try one of these ...

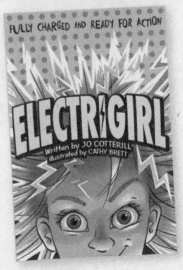